CW00447542

The Runaway Laundress

EMMA HARDWICK

COPYRIGHT

Title: The Runaway Laundress

First published in 2022

ISBN: 9798363915697

CONTENTS

Sophie Bryant 7

Poppy Patterson 27

St Regis Club 54

Patrick Gallagher 72

Lady Maria Gresham 83

Lord Anthony Gresham 91

The accidental meeting 94

Politics 106

Mr Aldridge 113

Miss Holmes 125

The invitation 138

The Lyon's Tearooms Piccadilly 150

Mr and Mrs Austen 164

Rumour 182

Despair 200

The heirs 210

Blackmail 220

The Doggett Arms 235

Give me the bag 248

Call Dr Goodwin 258

Loss and gain 270

1

SOPHIE BRYANT

Sophie Bryant gazed into the blackness of the night with tired eyes. She had never slept in a proper bed with a cast iron frame, mattress, and thick woollen blankets to keep her warm on those savage winter nights. The poor girl had been banished into the loft of her parents' hovel from the moment she was old enough to negotiate the ladder. She had slept there ever since. Neither parent paid any attention to the comfort of their daughter's quarters or the comfort of her soul.

A young Sophie lay in a humble bed pressed against the chimney wall, hoping in vain for warmth. A leak in the thatch caused water droplets to bounce off the attic floor. The drip-dripping made an irregular beat against the wooden planks, irritating her and keeping her awake. Wearing all the clothes she owned, she lay beneath a few layers of threadbare rags. She wriggled herself into the insulating hay, and although her resting place was rather prickly, she was warmer at least.

Sophie's eyes were wide open, and although she was staring at the thatch above her head, her mind was far away. Although Sophie knew that by fate, she had been born into the impoverished world of her parents, she refused to accept that this was her destiny. The young woman had dreams which were so tangible that she could feel them in her bones even if they didn't yet exist. Sophie Bryant knew that there was a bright future ahead of her. Why shouldn't there be?

*

Sophie stood at the rough bench that her mother called a kitchen table. Their evening meal would be a gnarled pork bone, a soft carrot, and two wizened potatoes.

"Look, ma," the girl smiled and chirped. "We're going to have a lovely dinner tonight.".

Sitting in an old bentwood rocking chair, Ada didn't answer her daughter. She swayed back and forth, hardly conscious of the baby nuzzling at her bosom.

"This will make you feel better, ma. It will give you milk for the little 'un," Sophie said, trying to make conversation.

"Leave me be, Sophie. Stop bothering me and cut yer yarning about the bairn."

"Only you can feed him, ma."

Sophie held back from delivering a despicable home truth, telling her mother that the others had all died due to her parents' neglect. There was no point. Ada Bryant didn't care. She had always lived in abject poverty and isolation on the moors, where the land offered no comfort or beauty. The sun shone dimly upon them in the summer, but for the remainder of the year, the weather was cruel. The vast grassy heathlands were punctuated by rocky outcrops, and there was seldom something to see on the horizon. The closest village was four miles west of their ramshackle dwelling.

Sophie's mother sat in front of the fire, nursing her seventh child. The girl had one eye on her mother as she cooked on the iron stove.

Ada had given birth to seven children over the last decade, but none had survived. Sophie had cooed and cuddled the first little creature and fallen in love with it. The little baby had been named Ann. One morning, Sophie found the tot blue and dead in Ada's bed. So young she couldn't comprehend that death was the end of life.

> "Ma! Ma! She's not waking up!" Sophie pleaded, but her mother didn't show any concern.

Ada first cut herself a piece of bread before dawdling over to check. She looked down at the dead infant and studied it while she chewed on her breakfast.

> "Aww, that's too bad for the little 'un then," she sighed. "Your pa will know what to do when he comes home. Just leave her there."

> "No, ma, no! She is cold. We must cover her up and keep her warm."

Sophie swaddled little Ann in a rough blanket, then sat in front of the dwindling fire. She stayed there all day trying to warm up her tiny sister, unbeknownst to her that the precious little thing would never wake up and that the blood in her little body had stopped flowing forever.

When Gerry Bryant got home, Ada pointed to the corpse Sophie still clutched and comforted. The young girl could have sworn she heard her father muttering delight under his breath.

> "There's no chance on God's green earth I'm paying Scott to bury it. You could have dug the hole, so you could have," he chastised Sophie. "Now, I've gotta do it meself in this blizzard," he complained.

Sophie spent days begging Ada for answers until her mother lost her temper and threw a heavy cast iron pot at her.

"Get ye gone, now," drawled Ada.

The girl returned to her chair, where she wriggled until she was comfortable and stared into the ether, blocking out a world she couldn't function in.

By the time the fourth baby died in the same manner, Sophie was immune to death. She didn't need to consult the tea leaves to know that this eighth baby would die the same way as all the others had. Ada no longer named the babies, and she was so unschooled that she couldn't count beyond five.

Ada was a simpleton. She had no personality or drive. Some people said Ada was retarded, while others joked that she had been beaten over her head as a baby. There were no formal diagnoses for Ada's condition, and the town gossip was that if she had been born in a city, she would have been classed an imbecile and put in an asylum.

She had met her husband, Gerry, at the May Fair. She had been slow and withdrawn. Her wide round face had smiled. Her eyes, set far apart, had shown light for a brief while. Her stubby puffed hands had struggled to put flowers in her hair in a hopeless attempt to make herself *'look like the other pretty girls.'*

Gerry Bryant was a serial opportunist. With six ales under the belt, he was more forward than usual. Ada's parents were drunkards who lived on the moors. They were an embittered, anti-social couple, and Ada was their only child, which was unusual for those times. She endured a solitary life. She had never attended school, so her only point of reference was what she observed in nature. Ada's desire for a partner was as instinctive as breathing.

Gerry Bryant had eyed the simple soul hungrily. The country girl who grew up in isolation had an innocence and vulnerability that he could sense, which appealed to him greatly. He stalked her like a lion as she walked around the fairground. He assumed from her manner that she was not like the other lasses in the village. By her eyes and stammer, he confirmed that she was not normal.

> "You're the prettiest girl at the fair," Gerry had said gently, exuding all the charm he was renowned for.

Ada blinked and smiled, her eyes vacant and distant.

> "Would you come with me to the May dance tonight?" Gerry cooed.

Ada nodded without a smile. Gerry put out his hand and touched her fat stubby one. She felt a tingling sensation rush up her arm, and the hair on her neck stood up with pleasure and arousal. From that moment, Gerry could have done anything, and Ada would have been a willing participant—and he knew it.

Gerry had been married before, and his first wife's death had been a mystery. The doctor declared that it was a confounding disease without a name that had finally taken her life. But, alas, it was Gerry's vicious fist in the abdomen that had seen her off. Blood had flooded into her body cavity, and she had haemorrhaged to death. Gerry set to work and buried her as soon as the doctor left and before the police arrived. When the investigator did arrive at the rural plot, they had no reason or desire to disinter the corpse. So, Mary Bryant, dressed only in her undergarments, rested beneath the cold, muddy earth, and her killer escaped justice.

The incident taught Gerry two lessons. It was easier to kill someone than he had imagined, and he had been lucky to escape the noose. He would never be that vicious again, but that wouldn't prevent him from beating his wife and child. He just went about it more gently. He was a natural bully and bombarded Ada and Sophie with insults. Ada was oblivious and vacant of emotion, but Sophie was of sound mind, and the words echoed through her soul for days after he had cursed at her.

> "Ye wee little wench," he would shout at her. "Just like ye useless mother, so ye are. Sick of mind. I rue the day she spawned you. I curse the day I allowed you to live."

Sophie was nothing like her mother, and his menaces terrified her. Although she was very young, there was something ominous about the threats. They were deep and dark and spoke of other things, things she would only realise when she was much older.

Ada's parents were as disinterested in Gerry as they were in Ada. The only thing that endeared Gerry to them was that he provided a steady flow of drink and coins each Saturday night.

> "Aww, Gerry, me lad," the old witchy mother-in-law would croon, "you shouldn't have gone to all this trouble. Ye know we are not heavy drinkers."

Before the words were cold in her mouth, she had already whipped the bottle from his hand and uncorked it.

His father-in-law would simply nod his head without smiling and put out his arm, then give an impatient shake of his wrist. His wife merrily filled his tin mug. It was the only moment of forced jolliness she would display until Gerry returned the following Saturday to replenish their stock.

The old couple looked as bitter as they were. Thin, bony, toothless, they almost danced a jig when Gerry asked their permission to marry Ada. His request was a godsend. It would be one less mouth to feed, and the 'celebrations' would be an excuse for a few more bottles of hellfire to dull them against the sentence of living.

There was always a string of marriages after the May Fair, and a hoard of babies followed nine months later. Ada and Gerry were no different. Ada was harmless, but she had no inkling of how to care for a baby. From the moment that her first child Sophie was born, Gerry realised that his wife was an inept mother. Her maternal instincts were poor, and there was nobody to teach her how to nurse a child. Gerry couldn't stand the incessant screaming of the hungry baby.

> "Shut the thing up," he would scream in Ada's face, but to no avail—she didn't know how.

He would grab Sophie from Ada and be tempted to smash her head against the wall in a fury, but the thought of how powerful his temper could be stopped him at the brink. Eventually, he begged his mother to help him. Granny Bryant lived six miles east in a huddle of houses called Acre's Catch. She was a humble yet bright woman. She was appalled by what she was met by at her son's house. The house was riddled with filth and pestilence. Granny Bryant was poor, but she had no time for dirt. At first, Granny Bryant was sympathetic, but she became increasingly frustrated watching her son and daughter-in-law floundering.

In the end, Ada left Granny Bryant to care for Sophie, and she never held her child again. If Granny Bryant had her way, she would have taken young Sophie to live with her, but Gerry refused to hear of it. The local folk already had a poor opinion of him. He needed to keep up the pretence that he and Ada were good parents.

"What will people say about us?" Gerry whined to his mother.

"You won't be the first to give up your child to be cared for by someone else."

"But people will talk, ma, and I still have me pride."

Granny Bryant could only shake her head. The more she argued, the more Gerry dug his heels in. Gerry knew that eventually, Sophie would reach an age where she would become useful. She could help on the plot or find work to support him and Ada, but he would suffer until then.

Granny Bryant died shortly before little Ann was born. She passed away peacefully in her sleep. Her body was exhausted, but her soul was at war.

Ada regressed to nothing more than an empty shell. She became a grown-up child giving birth to more children. Pregnant or not, nothing stopped Gerry Bryant from using his wife night after night.

The severely neglected Sophie kept the humble home clean. She scrubbed the floor, which had several stones missing. She washed her parents' clothes, fed the animals, and made simple food which was mostly bread and dripping. She had to use and reuse the tea leaves as Gerry's drinking was more important than his family's comfort. Gentle Granny Bryant had been a kind disciplinarian who had a steady routine of how housework should be done. As young as Sophie was, Granny Bryant's lessons were imprinted upon her mind. The tiny home was immaculate. Sophie wore clean rags, and she had pride in how she was perceived.

Dim-witted Ada was a lifeless, uncomplaining phantom who questioned nothing her husband did, giving him free rein to indulge in whatever pleasure he chose. Every night Gerry would reach home drunk. He would abuse the naked Ada for hours at a time until his desire was satiated, all the while unaware that Sophie could hear them.

*

Sophie stuffed her earholes with pieces of rag and sank into the hay bed, trying to ignore what was happening directly below her. She abhorred both her parents. They were so disgusting to her she couldn't meet their eyes when they spoke. Sophie had done her best to insulate herself from Ada and Gerry but to no avail. No matter how hard she tried, she couldn't render herself deaf or blind to what happened below.

It was Reverend Scott who had the courage to face Ada and Gerry Bryant after Sophie caused a significant furore in the village.

It was an icily cold Wednesday afternoon, and Sophie had taken a walk to the village to buy flour. Sophie loved going food shopping. It was an opportunity for her to dress up and escape the monotonous repetition of her daily chores. The villagers had empathy for the lass, who was poor but clean. Someone was always kind enough to donate her a pair of boots or a dress if they had something in dire need of repair going spare. Sophie refused to wear her good clothes at home, but when she went shopping, she made sure that she looked as smart as possible with the little she had.

She had transformed into a delicate, beautiful young woman. She was tall and slim with the fairest skin. Her hair was a strawberry blonde, and she had bright blue eyes. She had inherited none of her mother's mental defects and none of her father's poor character.

That day, Sophie was cold, flustered and irritated. The grocer's shop was full of people, sheltering from the icy weather, and the busy atmosphere made her feel claustrophobic. Freddy McMillin was also in a line, awaiting his turn to be served. Freddy was a notorious Scottish bully. At twenty-one, he was short and stocky but already had the brute force of a navvy of thirty. While waiting to be served, Freddy persisted in staring at young Sophie with an eye to courting her. With the hustle and bustle in the small shop, he purposely bumped into her and took the opportunity to feel her rear. He made sure that his hand lingered, and then he squeezed it. Instead of apologising for his behaviour, the horrid young man leant forward and whispered a crude remark into Sophie's ear.

"There is more of that for you if you want it."

The sound of the suggestion was as abhorrent as his breath, which stank of tobacco.

Sophie turned around and slapped him as hard as she could.

"Damn you, Freddy McMillin. You don't talk to me that way. Get you gone and keep yer filthy paws to yourself. I will kick ye in the knackers and then cut off yer knob if you dare touch me again," yelled Sophie at the top of her lungs.

With that, she kicked him in the shin as hard as she could. Freddy hunched over, cradling his leg. She had kicked harder than a dray horse.

A hush fell over the shoppers. The shopkeeper, Mr Brown, was mortified by her words and tone. All eyes were on Freddy McMillin as everybody wondered how the town bully would respond. Sophie had to wait for the flour, or she would have nothing to eat, so she stood her ground, refusing to run away. News spread about the village in literal minutes. Freddy McMillin limped out of town like a leper, furious that a nineteen-year-old girl had brought him to his knees.

"What is it, Mr Brown? Why are you looking at me like that?" Sophie demanded of the grocer.

"You used terrible language," answered Mr Brown.

"Freddy McMillan felt my backside. I don't like that. My pa feels me ma's all the time, so he does. I hate it. Now Freddy thinks he can do what he likes to me. It won't be his shins that get a good kicking. It will be his b—."

Sophie stopped herself, and Mr Brown didn't dare continue the conversation. Secretly he knew that Freddy deserved it but kept his opinion to himself. He was afraid that Sophie would continue her diatribe with even more colourful language than she had already displayed.

*

Sophie was furious. She walked home, kicking every stone she saw and crunching her heel into the icy puddles that had formed in the thick, rutted mud. It didn't concern her that she was damaging her best boots. She had a large stick in her hand, and every time she passed an evergreen hedgerow, she would beat the life out of it until the leaves sprang off the branches and landed about her like confetti. It was the only way to vent her wrath.

She passed Mrs Leary's cottage and took aim at the hedge outside. The woman shouted at Sophie to stop her tantrum, but the girl didn't stop but beat it even more.

> "What's got into you, Sophie Bryant?" Mrs Leary shouted, "I will give you a clout, so I will. Your father is going to give you a lashing when he hears what you've got up to."

The threat of a whipping brought Sophie to her senses, and she burst into tears. She was seldom in trouble, preferring to keep a polite distance and be disciplined in her conduct. Now, Mrs Leary was yelling at her and threatening her with her father. Mr Brown was beyond disappointed. She could live with her standards slipping. A few kind words and deeds would go a long way to repairing the damage done. However, Gerry Bryant was a different story. She was terrified when he wielded the strap and knew she was in for it.

It was well after dark when Sophie got home. News travelled fast, and Gerry had heard what his daughter had done.

He interrogated his daughter as if she had committed a crime and Freddy McMillin was innocent. Between tears and sobs, Gerry eventually got some of the story from Sophie.

“What did you say?” Gerry demanded of Sophie, while Ada sat on a chair, dazed and confused.

“I can’t say ‘em words. Don’t make me say them.”

Gerry stared down at Sophie as she blushed with shame.

“Tell me what you said, Sophie. I won’t be angry with you,” he demanded, but Sophie didn’t believe him.

“Well?” roared Gerry. “What did you say?”

Pushed to the limit, Sophie defiantly repeated verbatim what she had told Freddy McMillin at the grocery store.

Sophie clapped her hand over her mouth. She knew what was coming next. Her eyes were red, and her face covered in pink blotches.

With all his strength, Gerry lifted the strap, ready to bring it down upon her. Sophie watched. Everything was happening in slow motion. Gerry had beaten her for years. Whether she yielded to his punishment or faced him, the result would be the same. Freddy McMillin had outraged her. Her father was pouring fuel on that fire in her belly. In an instant, she decided she would no longer tolerate people doing as they pleased to her. For the first time in her life, she stood her ground and faced her disgusting father. She put out her hand and snarled at him.

> "Stop right there, Gerry Bryant. You should be beating Freddy McMillin for harassing me. But, instead, you will beat me. You're a coward. You have always been a coward. Do your worst, pa. It's all that you are good for."

Gerry Bryant's arm fell to his side, staring at his daughter. He couldn't decide whether to beat her to death or let her be. At least, not then.

*

The news of Sophie's outburst had also reached Reverend Scott's ears via the usual local gossips. He knew that he would have to go out to the Bryant cottage because when Gerry was furious and had a few drinks in him, he was capable of murder. Even though it was dark, he saddled his horse and made his way across the gloomy moor, wondering what to do for the best.

When the reverend knocked on the weathered front door, he could hear the commotion inside. He opened the door and what he saw peaked his anger. He watched Gerry Bryant leering over Sophie violently.

> "You need a good thrashing," shouted Gerry Bryant. "You have brought shame upon this house. You have not learned that vulgar language here. We are a well-respected family," Gerry Bryant lied out loud.

"Stop that right now, Gerry. You're an ogre. Don't go telling me otherwise. You have tormented the girl for years now," the vicar retaliated.

Reverend Scott was more a man of the world than he got credit for being. When he was out of his cassock, he had a wild temper, wild enough to match Gerry's.

"Stop it!" yelled Reverend Scott, failing to hide his fury. "Nothing will be achieved by beating her."

"Since when does the church deny a child a good hiding?" Gerry Bryant angrily demanded.

"Since *'the child'* is only repeating what she has heard her father say. Since *'the child'* is now a young woman. Since *'the child'* was defending herself against an opportunist reprobate." countered Reverend Scott in disgust. "She's not a child, Gerry. She's a young woman. A decent young woman until she's sorely provoked."

"Are you trying to suggest it's my fault just after saying she's old enough and independent enough to have a mind of her own?"

Reverend Scott was eager to give Gerry Bryant a good walloping, and he had to stop himself from swinging a punch at the drunken liar in front of him.

"I am saying you should have taken more responsibility for what your daughter sees and hears. Alas, it's too late, Bryant. The damage is done."

Ada sat on the rickety rocking chair, unable to communicate with anybody, her expression vacant. She just about followed the altercation, somewhat amused.

"What is wrong with Ada this time?" demanded Reverend Scott.

"It's just the way she is," answered Gerry sullenly.

"Is that a baby?" Reverend Scott pointed to the bundle of fabric in Ada's arms.

"Aye, another young 'un. Still hanging off her saggy old knorks, innit."

Reverend Scott grimaced. The crass reply enraged him further.

"Well, I hope you take better care of this one than you did, Sophie. Why was she never at school? Why have you never educated your child?" demanded the vicar.

"Now, don't you go starting on that, reverend. You know there was no money for that. And it's too late for all that bother now. The ungrateful little wench knows how to do chores. What more is there to know?"

"School was free."

"And who would help me with the work? I was always struggling to keep the place going and the bellies fed. Ada's neither use nor ornament."

Reverend Scott saw it wherever he went. Impoverished peasants worked their children to near death because they were too lazy to do it themselves. He knew that Gerry Bryant never lifted a finger to do anything.

"The girl will have to go into service. You're not capable of looking after her. Langford Manor has a position open for a young maid. I shall recommend Sophie for the post."

Gerry Bryant began to smile. It would mean an income for him.

"Don't look so happy, Gerry Bryant. She will earn very little at first, but she will be well looked after in the great house.

"Who'll look after the farm?"

"Perhaps you can motivate yourself to do some work?"

Gerry paced up and down, calculating the cost to his freedom if he lost Sophie's labour.

"She is nineteen, Gerry. She is old enough to go and work and earn herself a living," Reverend Scott told him.

Sophie stood up and stared at Scott, the thought of a chance to escape jolting her into action.

"I trust you have no objections, Sophie?"

"None!"

"Then, I have no choice," Gerry said dismally.

He turned to point at Ada and the child.

"What about the baby and her? Who will look after them when Sophie is gone?"

"You, Bryant! I shall inform the parish you might need extra help in the short run as you adjust."

Gerry knew Reverend Scott had the upper hand. It was a miracle that the authorities had not yet knocked on the door and arrested him for non-compliance with the Education Act or his poor record for keeping his children alive. The last thing he wanted was officials poking about in his affairs.

"If you do anything to Sophie when I leave, I will have you in court for cruelty. The judge will have you in prison without blinking an eye."

Gerry Bryant didn't argue. He knew that the vicar held all the cards. He couldn't risk appearing in court. He was terrified that his past would return to haunt him.

2

POPPY PATTERSON

Where other great houses in the area radiated dark antique gloom, Langford Manor was the complete opposite. It conveyed an atmosphere of light-heartedness. It was situated in the middle of an ancient woodland, and the grounds were large enough that the house never stood in the shadow of the trees. By night, the house's windows glowed with warm lamplight. By day, the bright flowers and variegated shrubs shone in the sunlit garden. The air was filled with the happy bustle of children, horses, and cheery staff going about their duties.

Sophie Bryant sat in Reverend Scott's carriage and took in the scene as it unfolded. She had never been anywhere close to a house of this magnitude before and was taken aback by the beauty surrounding her.

"It's wonderful," she whispered.

"It is only earthly goods, Sophie. Never confuse wealth and happiness."

"I have never seen a home like this."

"Don't get me wrong, lass. I am not extolling the virtue of poverty. It is fiction that it's better to be poor. Just remember that even the wealthy have their miseries as well."

Sophie was far too fascinated to participate in philosophical debate, and the vicar left her to admire the surroundings.

A jolly woman came bolting out of the front door with half a dozen children following her. One boy held a cricket bat, another a tennis racket.

"Reverend Scott, how nice to see you," yelled Lady Letitia in the most unladylike manner.

"Hello, Letitia."

She noted his use of her first name and smiled.

"Is this our new girl?" the woman trilled.

Sophie had been told that no servant would ever be greeted by the lady of the house, let alone be welcome to use the front door. It was all very confusing.

"Go and call Mrs Bethel," Lady Letitia instructed one of her sons.

"Yes, ma," the boy replied and dashed off to find the housekeeper.

Scott and Letitia engaged in polite conversation until Mrs Bethel arrived less than a minute later.

"There you are then. You must be young Sophie. Come along. Let me show you about," the housekeeper greeted her warmly.

Sophie picked up her ragged suitcase, followed Mrs Bethel and scuttled off down the long hallway.

"Shoo! Be gone, you lot," Lady Letitia ordered her offspring, waving her arm. "I want to speak to Reverend Scott privately."

When they were out of sight, the vicar spoke to Lady Letitia.

"She is a good girl, Letitia. Her childhood has not been favourable. She can barely read or write. I know that you have achieved miracles with everyone who works for you. I trust you can do it again."

"You embarrass me, vicar," she replied with a smile. "We just do what we can."

It was a beautifully sunny day, almost perfect. The sun baked down upon the house, and it was wind still. All the drapes of the mansion were wide open, and the welcoming yellow glow flooded into the rooms.

There was nothing pretentious about the interior. She counted four cats, and a tearaway puppy was chewing an unidentifiable object. Paintings of long-gone ancestors were dotted around, as would be expected, but the furniture was practical, and Sophie could see that it was well-used and not just for decoration. There was an occasional threadbare patch in the grand carpets by the doorways, and books were strewn on the settees and side tables.

> "Lady Letitia is an angel," Mrs Bethel told Sophie. "If you do your work, nobody will bother you. She refuses to have a miserable bunch of people around her, so don't be loathsome and grumpy, or you'll be sacked."

Sophie looked at Mrs Bethel with big eyes. She was not sure whether to believe the housekeeper or not.

> "Now, shall we introduce you to the others?"

Before Sophie could reply, she was whisked off to the scullery. The only person who was scary was Mr Pendennis, the butler. He spoke with a strange accent, and Mrs Bethel told Sophie that he was the only person in the house who got away with being stern.

> "If you offend him, he will report you to me. He is the eyes and ears of the household. Nothing gets past him. He is prone to bouts of being unreasonable, but we do our best to please him." Mrs Bethel explained with a laugh.

Sophie looked puzzled.

> "We make allowances, you see. His wife died two years ago, and he has never been the same. He is still grieving the loss. But who knows? Perhaps one day he will feel better and return to being jolly all the time?"

Sophie noted that the staff were working hard. Some waved. Others just lifted their heads briefly to flash a smile, absorbed in their tasks. Although there was a lot to accomplish in a day, the mountains of work completed were not motivated out of fear for their boss.

*

If there was any discipline to be meted out, that was done by Lord Langford.

A complete contrast to his wife, John Langford had been raised by a tyrant. His father was Lord Sydney Langford, a veteran of several colonial wars who had learnt the power of instilling fear. He didn't need the army to teach him to be cruel. He had discovered that all by himself.

However, at a young age, John Langford had decided that he would never rule over the folk on his land as his father did. John had never held a fondness for his father. His little respect for Sydney Langford was lost after witnessing his father flog a servant for stealing a slice of bread. The young John Langford had run upstairs to his bedroom and retched all over the bed, such was his horror at witnessing the event.

From that day forward, John Langford avoided the man who had sired him. His father was as good as dead to him. He succeeded in becoming invisible because he had six siblings, four of whom were sisters, whose lives Sydney loved to control with a view to strategically marrying them off to another family.

John was clever. He stayed out of trouble at school and spent as many holidays at his friends' homes as he could get away with. His sisters were a regular source of drama, and when they annoyed their wicked father sufficiently, he would lock himself in his cavernous study for most of the day as he planned how to deal with them.

John's eldest brother and first-born son, Leon, had died in his teenage years. A riding accident at the annual hunt had taken his life. The death of Lord Sydney Langford's favourite son had affected him severely. The boy had been his pride and joy. He had his father's mannerisms. He was ruthless and calculating and destined to go far.

Thus, by fate and not by destiny, John Langford succeeded his brother. The new incumbent at Langford Manor was determined not to follow in his cruel father's footsteps. He refused to perpetuate the man's brutal ways.

The young lord was an energetic man. He was quick to smile and make a joke, and his estate functioned well under his management, albeit chaotic. Lady Letitia Langford was his darling. He had met his future wife at a tedious soirée in Wales. While the other self-interested guests enjoyed the pomp and ceremony and were fixated on schmoozing their host, Letitia had escaped the tedium. John Langford had found her behind the house smoking. It was hardly befitting a lady to smoke, and thus John fell for her immediately, thanks to her irreverence. She had no airs and graces and no aspirations to marry. This made her even more attractive.

She took a drag from her cigarette in its long holder, and then her smoky breath revealed her plan for her life.

> "I intend to write and travel. The world is too big to suffer a stuffy house."

John could understand her desire for adventure. It was 1889 when they embarked on their secret world tour together. They were young, modern and in love. They travelled incognito, as ordinary folk, and few people sussed that they were a pair, let alone an aristocratic one.

It was the death of Lord Sydney Langford that interrupted their travels. While at the Cape Colony, John was notified of his father's demise. He was relieved that the tyrant had passed. He was also relieved that he had not had to stand next to the old man's bed and pretend that he loved the monster.

When John inherited his father's title, he took the opportunity to exercise his power and married the beautiful, vivacious Letitia Van Onselen of Dutch descent. The liberal woman was a commoner in her own country. The whole business could have evolved into a terrible scandal if John had bothered to pay any attention to it. But John didn't. He got on with being happy.

Behind her back, Lady Letitia Van Onselen Langford was often ridiculed and criticised for being too close to her staff, yet nobody dared tell her to her face. Whatever she heard about herself, she ignored. Lady Letitia was an intelligent, anarchic, jovial wonder.

On Letitia's first day at Langford Manor, she had studied the servants at a distance and then called for the butler and the housekeeper.

> "I can't bear to see the servants dressed in black every day of their lives. Call in the seamstress and choose a more cheerful colour. They are not going to a funeral or in mourning. Brighten them up. Please?"

After years and years of torment under Sydney Langford, Lady Letitia was a godsend. She had their quarters repainted. Squeaking doors were oiled, broken window latches repaired, and draughts excluded. Swathes of clean linen were purchased. Out went the threadbare blankets they had been sleeping under for decades. She heated the stable boys' rooms and fixed the leaks in the roof above their beds.

The insatiable wave of change swept through all the backrooms. At the same time, there was a significant transformation in lord's rooms too. There would have been mayhem were it not for the efficient housekeeper Mrs Bethel. For weeks before a party, weekend, hunt or ball, the great house was in a state of havoc. The best silver was brought out and buffed mercilessly. The cutlery was laid out immaculately. Flowers were arranged, curtains and rugs beaten clean, picture frames dusted, hearty fires stoked, delicacies cooked. The lord and lady of the house oversaw all the details, delighting in bringing out the best in their staff. Occasional mistakes were seen as an opportunity to learn and develop, not berate and belittle.

Because Lady and Lord Langford were of a younger, more forward-thinking generation, they had a different outlook on the world around them. They understood the value of education, hygiene, and household economics. They did their best to share these concepts with their staff. Some took the advice to heart and had they and their families had a better life experience. Others, although loyal, were not blessed with such curious minds and strong convictions to apply the advice. Everyone enjoyed a larger pay packet than was the norm. Life was difficult for the poor, and the Langfords refused to lose anyone to the hellish factories in the great cities. It was common knowledge that working at Langford Manor was a pleasure compared to the other estates, which meant finding loyal, hardworking staff was never a problem.

*

Sophie was awed by the size of the house. She couldn't believe her eyes when she saw the bed she would sleep in. It was a simple brass bed with a decent mattress covered with clean, blue-and-white striped fabric, a far cry from the prickly hay and rags she was used to. The sheets were white Egyptian cotton, and it was all covered by a thick, colourful eiderdown. In addition, there were two thick woollen blankets. In the corner stood a wood stove for heat. Sophie touched the linen. She ran her hand over the soft, cosy bedding. It felt like she was feeling heaven itself. All she wanted was for the day to pass so she could lie between the clean sheets. How wonderful it would be to rest there after a good day's work.

"Hey!" called a voice.

"Hey, what?" Sophie replied, flustered.

"First, bathe," instructed Poppy Patterson, her roommate.

"Bathe?"

"Yes," Poppy said, eyeing the grubby-looking girl in front of her. "Get into the bath and get clean."

Sophie stared at her wide-eyed.

"Have you never bathed before—? Blimey, you haven't, have you! Lady Langford has insisted on modern plumbing, bathtubs and a flushing WC."

Sophie shook her head. It was like she was being spoken to in a foreign tongue. She was too embarrassed to make eye contact with the other girl. Instead of ridicule, Poppy put her head back and gave a whoop of laughter.

"Oh good! We have something in common already." Poppy chuckled. "When I came here, I had never been in a bathtub either, and I thought the lavvy would swallow me whole. I am glad to hear that you are as unworldly as I was. I thought I was the only person who had never had a good wash before. I'm Poppy."

A slender hand was thrust towards the newcomer. Sophie took it and gave a small smile, unsure if she could yet trust the girl.

"Miss Sophie Bryant. Pleased to meet you. We only had an old tin bath at home," she confessed.

"Good on you, with your fancy lifestyle."

"Fancy?"

"Yes, we had to wash ourselves with a pail with an old rag as a sponge. Had to wash our clothes in it, and all."

"Really?"

Sophie was surprised at Poppy's candour.

"Why, yes! My family are desperately poor. My big brother and I are working, so things are a bit better for them nowadays."

"How many are in your family?"

"Ma, pa and four kids. Pete and I, then the two little ones."

Sophie nodded.

"And you?"

"Well, when I left, there was me, ma and pa with the eighth bairn."

"You're one of nine? Jeepers, your ma was pushing 'em out!"

Sophie's eyes fell.

"Not really. None of the others survived—"

"That's a story then."

"Yes," Sophie said softly.

"It must have been hard work and all looking after them babies. Well, until—you know."

Sophie didn't say anything. She suddenly felt sad.

"How old are you?" Poppy asked.

"Going on twenty-five," answered Sophie and blushed.

"Tell the truth and shame the devil, Sophie Bryant," Poppy told her playfully.

"Alright, I am nineteen. What of it? In two months, I will be twenty."

"I was just asking. I am twenty-eight,"

"You look nothing like it. Stop fibbing this instant."

Poppy tried to act serious and then broke into giggles.

"I am twenty-one," she spluttered as both of them laughed heartily.

Poppy was only two years older than Sophie, but it could have been ten. Poppy knew everyone and everything. She was shrewd and just the right side of cocky. She got away with a lot because she did everything with a smile on her face and a great sense of humour.

After they had bathed at night, Poppy and Sophie would climb between their clean white sheets. They spent hours talking in the small attic room that they shared.

"How is it that I never saw you at the parish school?" Poppy asked.

Sophie turned her head away and blushed.

"You don't need to be shy with me," Poppy said sincerely.

"I never went to the school."

"That's nothing to be ashamed of. So, you can't read or write? Can you do numbers?"

"I can count money, but I can't read."

"Well then, I will teach you what I know. But I promise you that it's not much."

*

Poppy was true to her word. She approached Mrs Bethel and asked to borrow a simple book from the nursery.

"Thought it might help me teach Sophie," she said. "In the evenings."

Mrs Bethel didn't think anything bad about the request. Sophie was not the first uneducated soul to enter the grounds, and it was good to know her place in the household had been given to someone who would seize the opportunity to blossom.

"Well done you, Poppy. What a kind soul you are."

Every night, Poppy would give Sophie lessons, and soon her underling was able to read simple books. Poppy had given her the most valuable treasure that she would ever receive.

When they blew out the lamp at night, Poppy's conversation usually centred around leaving the countryside and moving to the city. Her dream was to earn enough money to send home and to save. Although Poppy had more knowledge than her years counted for, she was a romantic. All she dreamed of was meeting a handsome young man of reasonable means, having a tiny home, and bearing children.

"How old do you need to be to go and work in the city?" Sophie asked naively.

"We could go now if we wanted to," Poppy whispered.

"Aww, be off with ye now. I'm still far too young to go anywhere. Besides, we get paid well here."

"Yes, but we're stuck in the middle of nowhere. Aren't you curious?"

"No."

"Well, you can stay on as long as you like," said Poppy. "If I find a job in London, I will leave tomorrow."

"Lady Letitia is very good to us," said Sophie, "and I don't want to go to the city. I've heard terrible things. I like it here."

"I will take you with me and look out for you, I promise. All I'll say is think of the fun we'll have with handsome husbands beside us. Theatres. Restaurants. We can even continue your education in a museum or library! Just imagine."

Sophie didn't want to imagine anything. She was unsure of herself. For the first time in her life, she had someone looking out for her instead of needing to be the neglected surrogate mother to seven dead children. She wasn't convinced, but Poppy had planted a seed in her unconscious mind. The suggestion that there was a life beyond Langford Manor would go on to intrigue her.

Sophie began to consider the future as the weeks rolled by. Poppy became ever more zealous in promoting the joys of city living as she realised she was wearing her colleague down and over to her way of thinking. When Poppy spoke, there was never any mention of poverty, crime, or cholera, simply the benefits of a higher standard of living and a chance for adventure with handsome husbands beside them. Eventually, Sophie became entranced by the prospect of seeing London first-hand.

"Have you ever been to London?" Sophie asked Poppy one night.

"No, no, never, but me Aunty Di was there. She went there on the train and found work in a shop. One of those swanky department stores in the West End. She helped dust all the products on the shelves and kept them all nice. That sort of thing. She cleaned the display windows on the inside too, which meant she could watch all the nice young men walk by. The old fella who ran it was like our lady here. He offered a good standard of lodgings with the job too. Built a big modern block just around the corner for all his workers to stay in. Like a housing trust would, I suppose."

"That sounds interesting. Tell me more." Sophie said, trying to coax more information from her.

Sadly, the information she elucidated from Poppy was all lies. There was an Aunty Di who had indeed gone to London—but, unbeknown to Poppy, she had ended up in Spitalfields washing bottles in an ale house and struggling to make ends meet in a squalid tenement.

"Did she like the department store?"

"She loved it. She couldn't speak enough about it."

"I still don't know," Sophie said cautiously.

"Mind you, Aunty was a dim-witted one. Only had one eye, so she did."

Poppy began to laugh.

"Aww, you're lying, so you are!"

Sophie was almost choking she was laughing so much.

"I'm not. They said that she would only clean one half of a display cabinet 'cos she couldn't see the other half," Poppy roared.

"Stop fibbing. This is important."

"Sorry," Poppy said, trying to regain her composure. "I have seen a lot of pictures of London."

Poppy's tone became more enthusiastic the longer she spoke.

"There are trains that work underground. Electric lights banish the darkness from the streets at night. Everybody dresses smartly, and there are a lot of shops. Best of all, with a few million people, there has to be somebody to fall in love with. You mark my words."

And that was the crux of Poppy's reasoning. She had confessed, at last, she wanted to be in love.

"I can't wait to get married, can you? A lovely tall, dark-haired chap. Clean-shaven but bushy sideburns. Strong jaw, obviously. Good sense of humour—obviously!"

As Poppy continued to eulogise, Sophie still was not convinced she needed to go as far as London to find a husband. Surely, good men lived locally too? Maybe one of the other male servants who worked on a far-flung corner of the estate might be the one for her? Although after a few months now, a young suiter had still not appeared.

Then she remembered her father was a local man. And then her mind drifted onto her ordeal with the odious Freddy McMillin when he tried it on. The humiliating episode enraged her all over again. The more she thought about it, the more it made perfect sense to at least investigate further before being hasty. Perhaps they could take a day trip to the city and meet Aunty Di to ask her how things were going?

To stay where she was, was to forever be exposed to the likes of all the Freddy McMillins in the area. On the lonely moors, the likelihood of finding a good unmarried man was rare, if not impossible. She began sifting through the list of families that lived around those parts in her head. There were no young men who qualified as good stock. They were already taken or young abusive drunkards.

She decided Poppy's suggestion may not be that unreasonable after all.

Sophie fell asleep dreaming of middle-class men in top hats and their wives in fine dresses. Her final thought was about the train. *'Who had ever heard of a train running under the deep underground? It's pitch black. There's nothing to see!'*

*

Poppy behaved like a person possessed, even though nothing of her plan had materialised. Sophie had given up fretting that she would soon need to decide to stay at Langford Manor or go to the great city of London.

It would go on to stay a dream until six months later.

Late one Sunday night, Poppy stormed into their room with a newspaper. She threw it onto the floor, fell to her knees and opened it at the small advertisement pages.

"Here, look at this," she ordered Sophie.

Poppy jabbed her finger at an advertisement she had ringed with a pencil.

"Read it, Sophie."

In a long column of text so small that it was a struggle to read, one advert had an ornate twirly frame around it. As small as it was, it stood out from the rest.

ST REGIS—PALL MALL
SEEKING LAUNDRY MAIDS

"What does this mean, Poppy? What's St Regis? It's not a convent, is it? And even if it is, it's not even in London!"

"Good grief, no! That's Bognor Regis! The St Regis is a famous club, and it's looking for servants—and we have a chance to apply for jobs. Pall Mall is one of the grandest streets in the whole of London!"

"They will never consider us, Poppy. Why would they choose two girls from the opposite side of the country?"

"I don't know, Sophie, but I am going to write to them and apply for the position. The worst that can happen is we get knocked back."

"Poppy, this is all happening too quickly. I need time to think," Sophie stammered.

"There's nothing to think about. I want a better life, Sophie. I want a husband and a family. I don't want to live in a hovel for the rest of my life, marry a shepherd and have twenty-five children," Poppy exaggerated.

Sophie giggled. It sounded hilarious when Poppy put it that way. Then the tone got more serious.

"If you think about it, they'll hire someone else at the club, and you'll miss out, ending up stuck here. Are my words so far-fetched? Look around us. Susan Cunningham. Clare Jones. Ellen Curtis.

All of them already have three or four babies, stuck in damp little cottages on the moors, the only highlight of the week going to Mr Brown's shop. Come with me," begged Poppy. "It would be wonderful if you did."

"Maybe," was all Sophie could muster for now.

She was terrified. She knew the time had arrived, and she had a decision to make. Poppy's finger continued to poke at the advert.

"They are offering more than what we are earning here."

"But there is free accommodation here. Rents in London will be sky-high!"

"Wrong. There is free accommodation included. We can share everything just like we do here. This is the opportunity that we have waited for."

Sophie's stomach was churning. It was a momentous decision, but everything that Poppy said made sense.

"You're old enough to make your own decisions," Poppy said, cranking up the pressure. "And no one has a more vested interest in your future success than you. I'm in. Are you in?"

It was this reasoning that sealed Sophie's fate. Sophie had learned early in life that making decisions to safeguard her own future had always worked out better than drifting and letting her parents decide for her. She had done well since she moved out of the family home. Moving to the city, with all the opportunities and new experiences, made sense.

"I am going to write to them on behalf of both of us," Poppy said firmly. "We can go for the interview, see how it goes, and then decide. If it feels wrong, we can come back. If it goes well—"

Poppy's eyes twinkled mischievously.

"Alright then. I'm in. Let's do it."

Poppy issued a considerable whoop, bolted from the room, and tore downstairs to find some paper and write their letter to the president of the St Regis Club, London.

*

It was the opening of the Christmas season, and the house held more guests than ever before. The crowd was a warm and joyous bunch, much like their hosts. They were accompanied by their unruly offspring, who had the run of the house. The staff spent most of the holiday weekend tearing about saving young hooligans from themselves and each other.

"Give them some leeway, Mr Pendennis," Lady Letitia advised the old butler kindly. "As long as they are not vandalising the property, please allow them to be happy."

"They have removed the damask curtains from Master Paul's bed because they are building a stage for a Christmas pageant. They plan to present it on Christmas Eve."

Lady Letitia didn't want to imply that Mr Pendennis was a nag. She had to show her faith in him,

"Mr Pendennis, that is preposterous. I will send Nanny Porter to take control of the situation. Perhaps she can find some old drapes, and they can have their fun with those instead."

The butler left Lady Letitia's company feeling vindicated. He adored his mistress, and she, in return, couldn't do without him. It was a perfect example of Lady Letitia's genuine love for people.

*

The children who were not participating in the pageant had escaped outdoors. It had snowed. The grass was now a fluffy white blanket. The slushy paths squelched as they were hammered by their little feet. It had been cold enough that a thick layer of ice lay over the pond at the far end of the formal garden. Sophie had been tasked to take four boys down to the pond and watch them skate. Why Lady Letitia had chosen her for the job was a mystery, Sophie could neither skate nor swim. If there was an accident, she would be hopeless at rescuing anyone.

"Oh, just fish them out with a stick or something, then rush them home and plonk them in front of a fire," said his lordship when she mentioned her shortcomings.

Sophie was dressed in many layers of clothes, and the brisk walk had warmed her up in no time. She had no sooner reached the small ornamental gazebo that stood next to the pond than she heard Poppy yelling behind her.

"Sophie! Look here."

She saw the young woman running toward her waving something in the air.

"What is it?" Sophie called out.

"We've been accepted, Sophie. They want us."

"Seriously?"

"Yes! They want us."

Poppy was huffing and puffing from the run through the snow before wheezing the news to her friend.

"They actually want us. In London. Both of us, they have accepted both of us."

Sophie's eyes were wide. She didn't know what to say. It was all so sudden. It had only been a few days since they sent their application.

"When?" Sophie whispered. "What about the interview? What about us seeing if we liked it first?"

"We don't need to bother with all that rigmarole. We just have to deliver ourselves there on the 1st of January."

Poppy unfurled a leaflet with an illustration of the impressive property

"Look at the place! We'll be so happy here!"

Her face broke out in a broad smile, and she hugged Sophie.

"I can't believe it," Sophie laughed nervously, eyeing up the grand portico and the huge windows.

"It's a new chance! A new life! A new world! Our dreams are finally all coming true!"

Poppy joyfully danced and rejoiced in the snow. It was a scene that would be imprinted on Sophie's mind forever.

*

The resignation of the two girls caused consternation among the staff. Their decision was escalated from Mrs Bethel to Mr Pendennis. The butler, horrified, reported the matter immediately to Lady Letitia, who then told her husband.

Despite the season's frivolity, the two young women were summoned to Lord Langford's study. For once, he was sterner than his valet.

"The St Regis Club?" John Langford whispered quietly. "*The* St Regis Club?"

"Have you heard of it, John?" asked his wife.

"No. It must be new."

He stared into space, wondering what was going through the girls' minds. Why would they want to work in a place full of stuffy old men?

Lady Leticia wrung her hands together as she spoke.

"Do you know anything about working in a men's club in the middle of London? Neither of you have set foot there. It's a different world to ours. Here you are protected."

John picked up on her concerns.

"You're too young to be exposed to those horrible old British relics. I have heard terrible tales in the newspapers of girls being taken advantage of. They end up more like prisoners than staff. They might have a roof over their heads, but when they have their wages withheld, they are at the mercy of the club owner to employ them as they wish. They are expected to do a lot more than laundry."

John's voice trailed off as he ran out of things to mention that could change their minds. He could see he was getting nowhere.

Neither Poppy nor Sophie understood why they were that concerned. They were liberated people of the world. How was it that they could be so shocked? What was the worry if they ended up serving vol-au-vents at posh parties?

"We will pay you more to remain here," Lady Letitia begged. "An extra two shillings a week."

John Langford raised an eyebrow.

"Why do you want to leave?" he asked so gently he could have been talking to one of his children. "You earn a good income here."

"We want to see the world, your lordship," Poppy said honestly.

Lady Letitia slumped back in her chair. She was not one for drama, but she was struggling to keep her composure. She understood how they felt. She had been in the same position, but she was protected by her social class. These girls were working class, even maybe less than that, because they had no experience apart from their time at the manor. Working-class city women were far more shrewd about surviving such harsh conditions. They could handle an army of men ready to prey upon them for their own ends. She feared these two youngsters would be slaughtered like lambs.

"We can't stop you from seeking adventure. I was the same at your age. You have our blessing, but you have to promise me that you will return to Langford Manor if you are ever in trouble. There will always be a place for you here."

3

ST REGIS CLUB

Sophie and Poppy could only afford a third-class train ticket to London. Sophie spent all her savings on the ticket and almost cried when she handed over the money to the clerk.

The two young women shared a compartment with a family with five children. They were all squashed against each other uncomfortably. The children fought and squabbled throughout the entire journey, and one travel-sick child made a mess of his mother's lap.

All the third-class compartments were so full that there was nowhere to escape. Sophie and Poppy had to suffer in silence, but they both secretly wished that the little blighters would fall out of the window.

They reached London exhausted but safe. Waterloo station was large and imposing, the immense steel and glass structure both wondrous and terrifying, as fragile looking as it was strong.

They were engulfed by waves of travellers who were passing through the station and welcoming loved ones. Sophie had never seen so many trains or people. The large arched roof made them feel like ants, with the passengers dwarfed beneath it.

The chaos of Waterloo belied its efficiency. Porters pushed large luggage trolleys about, both delivering and collecting passengers' suitcases, hat boxes and chests. Whistles blew, and conductors yelled while passengers trudged up or down the platforms depending on where they were in their journeys.

Sophie was in awe of everything around her. She jumped when she heard the screech of an engine's driving wheels as they began to turn, and steam bellowed out from under the locomotive, threatening to engulf her. Giggling, Poppy pulled her friend to safety, her knees threatening to buckle with amusement. Sophie's were about to collapse with terror.

The two young women tried to look confident as they breezed down the steps that led to the main road outside, each carrying a small suitcase which held all their earthly belongings.

Sophie looked about, and she began to feel embarrassed. She had picked out her best dress, but it was shabby, dull, and old-fashioned compared to what other ladies had to wear. They both stuck out like country mice on the sophisticated streets of London.

Poppy noted her friend's face and had to laugh.

"One day, we will dress like that," Poppy said, pointing at a young woman wearing an impeccable outfit. "We will be the talk of the town and the belles of the ball."

It was good to dream, but Sophie was realistic. She felt Poppy's prediction was unlikely to materialise.

They crossed the busy wide bridge across the Thames to the opposite embankment.

A myriad of roads led from the bridge at the far side. A bewildered Sophie looked at Poppy.

"It's alright. I know where to go. We follow the road with the river on our left-hand side until we reach the Houses of Parliament. Then we're nearly there. We can ask someone about the last bit."

A newspaper seller on Parliament Square advised them to walk down Whitehall and Northumberland Avenue until they saw Trafalgar Square.

"Turn left when you get to the square, then you're on the Mall. There's something going on up there today, so keep a good hold of your suitcases."

"Thank you, sir. And, I think I'll take a paper," said Poppy parting with most of what remained of her money.

As they approached Trafalgar Square, Sophie was mesmerised by the size and splendour of the memorial to Nelson. It towered above the neighbouring buildings. She had heard talk of the column, but the reality of its surroundings was far grander than any engraving that Poppy had shown her.

Sophie looked at the magnificent buildings en route and suddenly remembered how awful she looked in her tatty old clothes. She pulled her shawl tightly around her, feeling lowly, dowdy and self-conscious amongst all the finery.

As they approached the square, there was the sound of raised voices accompanied by flag waving.

"What's going on, Poppy?"

"Perhaps we're about to have our first adventure earlier than we thought?" she said with a grin.

The bystanders lining Northumberland Avenue seemed to wait with a considerable amount of apprehension, as did Sophie. Some of the tearooms and shops had closed their shutters. Bobbies were directing the cartmen and cabbies away from the square.

The girls noticed the square's right-hand side was filled with many working-class people.

"What's happening," Poppy asked an onlooker.

"London's Lord Mayor's just about to pass through in his state carriage," was the reply.

"That sounds fun," Poppy whispered to her anxious friend. "Free entertainment!"

The procession had started from the Guildhall at a quarter-past twelve. When the mayor left the prestigious building in the state coach, he was cordially greeted along the route by the members of the livery guilds. He reached the Royal Courts of Justice at two o'clock without incident, where he swore his allegiance to the city. The ceremonial route passed down the Strand and Charing Cross. The crowds had been growing steadily around the square, which was now thickly dotted with police.

> "Are they all here to see the mayor," Sophie asked a man. "I don't think I've ever seen so many people in one place!"
>
> "No, miss. One of the trade unions had chosen to use the gathering for its own ends. Keeps the coppers guessing what they're up to."

Sophie felt very much out of her depth. Poppy was on tip-toes to get a better view of the policemen in their smart uniforms.

The officers made no effort to stop the people who crowded round Nelson's monument, dozens of whom were now climbing up to the top of the pedestal and waving small red flags.

Poppy saw a man amongst the flagbearers speaking to the crowd, but he didn't appear to create much of an impression, his voice inaudible over the din. Another speaker, on the east side of the pedestal, speaking into some sort of metal cone held up to his mouth, was addressing another group of people with much more success. Loud shouts and cheers filled the air that was punched by fists from below.

Suddenly, a commotion broke out, caused by the appearance of a small troop of Horse Guards, who had marched their steeds down Whitehall and into the square. Their presence made a visible impression on the crowd. Many of them made off as quickly as they could, not wishing to get trampled under the horses' hefty hooves.

"We should get out of here, Poppy!" Sophie pleaded, pulling her friend by the elbow.

Poppy nodded, and the two women forced their way towards Pall Mall, fighting their way across a sea of bodies.

The guardsmen rode towards Nelson's column. The people who had occupied its pedestal fled in all directions. The police moved about in large bodies, their elbows locked, scattering the crowds in all directions.

A few of the rougher sort among the crowd made a slight show of resistance, mainly hurling insults at the officers, but soon they were compelled to submit to the superior force. The Horse Guards paraded through the square, clearing the roads ready for the cartmen to pass through once more.

The women heard one of the ringleaders order the crowd to make their way to Downing Street to demonstrate in front of the Prime Minister's house. Another man advised some stragglers to meet up at the bandstand in Hyde Park for another public debate.

The women were carried along the crowd as it flowed down Pall Mall, like two dandelion seeds taken in the breeze.

Poppy pointed to a sign saying "Duke of York Street". They stuck out their elbows and barged their way to freedom with determination.

"Well, that was fun!" Poppy trilled to Sophie, who was speechless. "And did you see the uniforms!"

"That's enough excitement for me for one day—actually one week," lamented Sophie with a weak smile as she dreamed of unpacking her belongings in their new lodgings and settling down to a quiet cup of tea.

A few strides later, they found themselves in the picturesque St James Square, which was quickly circumnavigated, Sophie's lack of self-worth magnifying with each step.

Poppy stopped in front of a Georgian-styled cream building. The sizeable imposing façade was dominated by decorative Doric pillars taller than any tree Sophie had ever seen. The two young women made for the heavy glossy black doors. They had only reached the second of ten steps when the concierge stopped them.

"What do you think you are doing? Get away from here!"

"We have to report for duty, sir," Poppy answered.

"You should not be on this street, let alone these steps."

He pulled up his nose as if they stank.

"Well, where do we get in?" Poppy asked naively.

"Take this lane to the left. Then turn right into the service alley. You will see a yard with a sign saying 'Servants, St Regis'. Never come this way again, or I will have you sacked."

Sophie and Poppy scurried away. The last thing they needed was to lose their jobs before they started.

"He was an unfriendly type. Makes old Mr Pendennis look full of sweetness and light," Poppy remarked, and they both giggled.

They followed the route that the concierge had given them and reached the sign above the thick wrought-iron gate. Under the words, someone had added a sketch of a skull and crossbones. The unwelcoming alleyway was menacing, ominous, and eerie, but neither girl wished to discuss their secret unease.

*

Sophie rang the bell, and they waited. Nobody arrived. Poppy rang the bell again, and a man appeared. He was dressed in a pitch-black uniform, so dark he melted into the gloomy, soot-stained servant's entrance.

"What do you want?" he snarled.

"We are the new maids," Poppy said, fumbling for the letter in her pocket.

She gave it to the man who read it.

"Follow me."

The big iron gate slammed shut behind them as if they were now prison inmates. Without another word, he led them to an entrance and waved them in.

"Sit down there," he pointed to a heavy wooden bench.

His tone had a chill to it. The man was as cold as the room that they were sitting in.

Sophie could feel goosebumps developing on her arms and behind her neck, but they were not caused by the cold. The curious bench they sat on was more like a church pew than a piece of household furniture, but the black and white floor tiles were more opulent, with hundreds of glittery little speckles twinkling at them.

"Do you think that we should stay here?" Sophie whispered. "It seems a bit—creepy?"

"Creepy? All we did was go up the wrong steps and get told off. Calm down," Poppy muttered, clearly irritated by the question.

"I don't like the feel of this place. Do you have any money on you? I used the last of what I had to get my ticket."

"You're not planning on running off, are you? Splitting on me the day we get here?"

"No," Sophie lied.

"Me neither. These are posh city people. Perhaps, it's just their way. You know how snooty these types can get. I bet they'll always look down at us country bumpkins until we learn the ropes."

Poppy secretly shared her concerns, but she didn't want to cause any more alarm. Sophie hoped that Poppy's explanation was the truth, or she would run away as soon as she received her first week's wages.

They waited for two hours before they saw the first signs of life. A pasty-looking maid approached them. She was also dressed in pitch black from head to toe. Her black hair was pulled back severely off her face, and a thick white line of scalp emerged where it was parted in the middle. Her eyes were large black orbs in her round snow-white face. Even her lips were white.

"Follow me."

The two words punctuated the silence, and then they disappeared ghostlike into the ether.

It seemed to Sophie that all these servants had no more than a handful of words in their vocabulary.

The girl stopped at a door with a sign that read 'housekeeper'.

"Leave your suitcases here."

Sophie and Poppy looked at each other confused.

"Sorry, what was that?" Poppy asked.

"Leave your suitcases here. Mrs Tremarie, the housekeeper, will inspect them. If there is nothing contraband inside them, you will receive them back shortly."

Expecting the women to comply immediately, the servant made her way towards a long corridor. Sophie whispered:

"If we pawn our cases, we could get the train fare home? Come on."

Before Poppy could answer, the sinister woman returned, indicating for them to follow her.

"If you will, just do as I ask. Thank you."

Neither girl wanted to leave what little they had but felt they had little choice. If the maid called for help, things would only get worse.

The spectral woman took them to the back of the building and led them up two flights of stairs. They found themselves in another corridor lined with more black and white chequered tiles. Everywhere was cold and clinical. There were no soft furnishings apart from dark drapes on the windows. As they walked, the young woman lectured them.

> "The women live on this floor. There will be no noise or cavorting. Your day will begin at five o'clock in the morning and end at eleven o'clock at night. Your lamp will be extinguished by eleven-thirty. If you don't adhere to these rules, you will be dismissed immediately."

Poppy and Sophie nodded.

> "This is a gentlemen's club. You won't venture further than the areas that you are assigned to. There is no excuse for entering the club for any reason. Is this clear?"

They nodded.

> "There is a 'no entry' sign on every door leading into the main body of the building."
>
> "What if we make a mistake?" Sophie asked.
>
> "Mistakes are not tolerated."

They stopped at one of the black doors in the corridor. The young woman took a key out of her pocket and opened it. Poppy and Sophie stepped in the room and were aghast. There were no proper windows, just a tiny opening barely four inches high by two feet wide. It was like a cell. There were two cupboards and two basic metal beds like the ones for soldiers in their barracks. There was no wash bowl.

> "The bathing facilities are down the hall. Patterson is assigned as a housemaid. Bryant, you are appointed as a laundry maid. You will report for duty at 5 o'clock tomorrow morning. You will hear the wake-up bell fifteen minutes before. Don't be late."

The two girls nodded again, too intimidated to utter a word as the young woman closed the door behind her.

*

Work in the St Regis Gentleman's Club differed greatly from what the two girls had experienced at Langford Manor. There was none of the easy camaraderie between the servants. There was a distinct class structure below the stairs which they would need to learn to navigate fast. All they knew for certain was that they were the lowliest amongst their peers and were constantly reminded of it. Even the food they had to eat was left over from the other servant's plates, not even the dining room.

Sophie collapsed on her bed in a flood of angry tears.

> "How long are we going to be trapped here, Poppy?"

"I feel so bad dragging you down here," said a remorseful Poppy. " I wanted to take you on an adventure—but it's ended in disaster."

Poppy tried to put a reassuring arm around her friend's shoulder, but it was coolly pushed away.

"Do you think that Lord Langford would have us back?" Sophie asked somewhat rhetorically.

"You heard them when we left. They will have us back."

"Please let us go back," begged Sophie. "This place is dreadful. It's only been a few days, and I'm at my wit's end."

"Tell you what," Poppy whispered behind her hand, "let's work the month out, just until we get our first pay packet, then run off. That way, we can afford to buy the train tickets home, and we won't have to travel like paupers. It's embarrassing enough that we will return to Langford Manor with our tails between our legs without going third class." Poppy suggested, trying to lighten the mood, but it was no use.

"Fine. But be warned, I am going home at the end of the month with or without you," Sophie said firmly. "It is not the work. I know how to work hard. It's the people. They are horrible—and they are horrid to each other. A bunch of lazy rotten backstabbers, the lot of them."

"Oh yes, and did you see how Mr Doubell, the French chef shouted at Millie Stern about peeling that carrot? We've got each other, and we can take some comfort in watching the madness unfold. We'll soon be free, laughing and joking with Mrs Bethel and Mr Pendennis. You'll see. Keep your chin up, girl."

As their conversation took on a lighter note, they both felt better for deciding to leave. If only they knew that wouldn't be possible.

*

As a laundress, it was Sophie's job to ensure there was a constant supply of boiling water as there were endless piles of dirty clothes, linen, and tablecloths, which needed laundering. She busied herself carrying large cast iron pots of boiling water from a colossal black stove that stood in the middle of the laundry to a big galvanised wash tub at the far end. Ordered to heat and move almost a hundred gallons of water a day. The work was never-ending.

Managing the great cauldrons sounded more straightforward than it was. The large building had piped water to fill them, which was a godsend, but the water still needed heating on the fire. Keeping the fire alight meant a lot of shovelling of coal. Then, the coal scuttles needed topping up constantly with more supplies. She was on the move for the entire shift.

After she had ensured that all the basins were full of steaming liquid, she would go to the large wooden tubs and begin to scrub. It would take a long time before the new recruit would ever be promoted to the more humane duties higher up the pecking order, such as starching and ironing. If she took a breather to recover from the strain of her toil, she would get an ear-bashing from a more senior servant.

It was winter, and within a few days of working, her hands were raw and covered in chilblains. The raw salt and carbolic soap needed to clean the linens burnt like fire, which added to her misery. Every night she would rub sheep fat into the open cracks, but there was no telling yet if it would make a difference.

By the time Sophie had been there for a week, she already understood how everything in the laundry worked. She had a pile of suits to get through, and washing them was a long delicate process. If she ruined one fibre on a Savile Row suit, her pay would be docked. She also had to be precise that she didn't mix up the suits. If she did, Mrs Tremarie had warned her she would lose her day off.

She picked up a suit and read the label affixed to one of the button holes. *'Lord Gresham, Room 17, 4th Floor'*. The clothing belonged to a medium-set man. A cloth label inside said the garment was made of mohair. She had been advised mohair was an expensive wool imported from Turkey and not to be washed in water hotter than ninety-degrees Fahrenheit.

One of the other girls had mistakenly boiled a badly stained mohair suit, and the prized garment had shrunk to half its original size, leaving it only fit for a man of Tom Thumb's stature. The mistake was hilarious for the other heartless staff, but young Clemmie Sutton had to forego two months' wages and all her Sunday afternoons off for nearly a year.

Sophie first put the dark jacket into tepid water to soak gently, then she put the trousers and waistcoat into another. She was annoyed when she saw the water turn pink, wishing that the kitchen would stop serving beetroot so often. No matter how cultured their lordships were, they were still messy eaters at times. Thankfully, the stain was not on a crisp white shirt collar, or the mark would have been impossible to remove.

Sophie's face was damp with perspiration from standing over the cauldrons, and her light red curls had escaped her bonnet and were sticking to her forehead. She looked the worse for wear.

It was seldom that the laundry received visitors, but she saw a shadowy outline of a man through the steam. As he came closer, she identified him as Patrick Gallagher. The Irishman was about thirty years old and the only cheerful soul in the building.

The housekeeper, Mrs Tremarie, rued the day the club employed the man. She resented his indomitable spirit and cheerful disposition, expecting the formality of the club to extend to its employees. She would have preferred that the young man be as sombre as an undertaker. Unfortunately for Mrs Tremarie, nothing could erase Patrick Gallagher's humour, kindness, or joy. She resented him even more because he was from the Emerald Isle and considered him lowly.

The prejudiced housekeeper didn't know that Patrick Gallagher was a highly qualified young man, employed for his brilliant ability to maintain the accounts and detect inconsistencies in the ledgers. He had a high position as the chief accountant, with many clerks working for him. He had control of all the accounts accrued below the stairs. In fact, he managed the finances of the entire club. His task as an accountant was far more valuable to the club than the irritation he caused Mrs Tremarie. It irked the woman that he had the approval of the board to override any decision she made.

When Patrick first arrived at St Regis, the miserable Mrs Tremarie had made various calls for his dismissal, but her requests had fallen upon deaf ears. Gallagher was trusted implicitly by the bigwigs. The aristocracy who appointed him knew that trustworthy, talented commoners were hard to come by.

Patrick Gallagher pushed his way through the laundry maids, ironers, and wranglers. Finally, he stood in front of Sophie. He smiled down at her. As Poppy had commented some days before, Patrick Gallagher wasn't half bad looking.

4

PATRICK GALLAGHER

Patrick Gallagher's parents had been humble fishermen from Ballyliffin, County Donegal. It had been a miracle that the Gallagher clan had survived the Great Hunger that began several decades earlier. Grandpa Gallagher and his sons were hardened fishermen used to living on the cold Atlantic coast. They toiled day in and day out to provide for their family, supplying the local market with fish. Sadly, as the famine became more severe, the local working population didn't have enough money to purchase food, and its prices steadily rising as the shortages cut deep. In the summer, they caught any fish that could feed them. In the winter, they caught crab. During the famine, the Gallaghers survived on whatever they could catch and scratch off the ragged rocks. It was not unusual to find kelp, limpet and mussel stew in their cooking pots. Generosity and love kept them and their neighbours alive as the community rallied together to share everything they considered food.

Granny and Grandpa Gallagher died in their beloved Donegal in the mid-forties, and it was sometime in the 1860's that Patrick's father, Iain, had fled to Liverpool, hoping to find work in a factory and to provide a more comfortable life for his wife and children.

Alas, England's northern industrial cities were more of a nightmare than Ireland. The Gallaghers had crossed the Irish sea, moving from one hell to another. Amongst all the dark, squalid buildings, they longed for home, the mystical land of Ireland with its emerald green grass, moody lakes, and ancient castles.

The promise of work in the great cotton mills had lured Iain Gallagher to Liverpool. Thousands of Irishmen queued in front of factories, hoping the foreman would come out and choose them for a job. With so much competition, it was slim pickings.

Someone had told Iain that there were more opportunities in Manchester, so he moved his family further up the Mersey and into the Irish quarter, which also happened to be the worst slum in England.

As prophesied, Iain found steady work, but it took three months to secure. At first, he was hopeful and enthusiastic when he started work at the cotton mill, with a simple job as a sweeper. The pay was poor, but it would put a bone and a loaf on their table at night. What was left over would be paid to the landlord, a mean corrupt man who rented out the filthy, foetid tenements. Iain was sure they would have been closed down immediately if the inspectors dared to venture into such dangerous territory. Gangs ruled the roost there, not the authorities.

The environment that Iain Gallagher had to work in was deadly. Moving from Donegal's fresh coastal air to

Salford's polluted air took its toll on Iain. The minute bits of fluff in the air soon clogged his lungs with dust and cotton. Iain Gallagher would have had a long life if he had remained in Donegal, but he died at the age of thirty-eight in the slums of Manchester.

Watching her husband die, impoverished and suffocating, had made Dilly, his wife, bitter. She hated the English for forcing them from their beloved home and into a living hell. The only way to cope was to throw her heart and bereft soul into their young son, Patrick.

Patrick Gallagher grew up without possessions, but he had a mother who fought like a demon to keep him safe and alive. He would have to wait until he was five to receive his first pair of third-hand boots. Until then, his mother had tied oily rags about his feet to keep them warm.

Being a slight child, Dilly had to fight tooth and nail to prevent him from being recruited as a chimney sweep.

> "Come now, Dilly, flower, be reasonable. You need the money. He's the right size for the job too. Could make a fortune, he could. Trust me."
>
> "Get away from me, Dicky Craven. My boy will never go down a chimney as long as I live. He is in the ragged school, and there he will stay. Even if I have to drop me undies down at the docks to keep a roof over our heads."

Unbeknownst to Patrick, that is precisely what she did. Even then, to make ends meet, Dilly and Patrick lived with sixteen other people in an airless room. Secretly, his mother would have returned to Ireland with him, but she couldn't scrape together the money for the ferry.

Worse than the poverty was that they were persecuted for being Irish. Not only was it their nationality that made them targets, but also their religion. They were Catholics. Patrick's mother didn't pay much heed to religion, but she did insist that Patrick went to Sunday School, and she would march her tiny son up the hill to the dismal St Michael's, where he received extra lessons. Dilly exploited every free school that she could find for Patrick.

Although the rest of the family she lived with baulked at him being educated in a protestant school, Dilly never wavered. Her son would have an education, whatever the cost.

> "As long as I provide my share of the board and lodgings, I will send me Patrick where I like," she argued.

Against all odds, Dilly Gallagher sacrificed every penny she had to educate Patrick. Her brother, Stephen, had gone into a rage.

> "The boy should be out earning his keep, not having an easy life up in that school. He should be making his own living at this age."

"I bring home enough money. Don't you go wagging your finger at me," Dilly shouted. "I earn enough to pay for all of you, so I do!"

By this time, everyone had guessed exactly how Dilly was earning enough money. Patrick was mortified.

"You can't, ma! Ye can't do it," Patrick had pleaded.

"Whether you go to school or not, I will still do me job, so I will."

"You're a common harlot, Dilly Gallagher! Do you hear me?" screamed her brother. "And you act like the brat is more special than the rest of us. Filling him with airs and graces like a toff."

"I will see to it that he is educated, even if I die doing so."

"You're a stupid woman, so you are. Damn you, Dilly Gallagher,"

Stephen lost his temper and threw their sparse furniture around the room until the already rickety chair was rendered forever useless.

"By the time he has finished learning, he will earn a good wage. More than any of us could. Then I will laugh in your face, and you will eat your words."

He had never had such a strong desire to hit his sister, having never lifted a hand to a woman, even in his drunken moments. This time, it took all his strength to keep his fists at his sides. Stephen never crossed Dilly again, and Dilly never gave in to him.

Patrick found his first decent-paid job as a clerk at a chandler on the docks. The first thing he did was rescue his mother from the local boozer where she worked, servicing customers behind the bar and in the back alley.

> "No more, ma. Never again, not while I am alive. You will never sell yourself again. I will look after you until the day I die. I will find you a fine little room. It will be clean and warm."

Although grateful, Patrick was deeply ashamed of what his mother had to sacrifice for him. He was often wracked with guilt, and every time he lifted his pen, he wished he had climbed down those Manchester chimneys, even if it had killed him.

The young man lived up to his promise to his mother. Dilly spent her latter years content and at peace. It was dirty water that eventually took her. She contracted cholera from an infected pump. Patrick looked after her until her last breath. Although the medicine was modern, Dilly's hard life had made her old before her time, and she died in Patrick's arms. Irrespective of the risk of contracting the disease, Patrick kissed Dilly on the forehead.

> "I love you, ma. I will make you proud."

"I know you will, son." Dilly had whispered, her voice raspy. "Go on and be happy."

Dilly closed her eyes one last time. She lasted for a few more hours, and then she passed. Her last breath was peaceful, just a sigh.

*

Patrick felt empty. He had no wish to stay with his Uncle Stephen and the rest of his Irish brethren. He knew he owed Stephen for the years he had not contributed and gave his uncle a monthly stipend. He would have fared better if he kept the money, but Patrick was proud. He would never allow Stephen the opportunity to insult him or taunt him with the sacrifices his mother had made. Besides, now he was older, Stephen found getting day labouring jobs more difficult to secure, so Patrick's contribution made for a good pension.

The great city of London lured Patrick away from his job in the chandlers. He was desperate to escape the memories of the past. There was no longer anybody in Lancashire for whom he cared. His spirits were low, but he still had ambition.

The striving young man took the train to London, travelling almost the same route as Sophie and Poppy. Within a week, he had found work as a clerk for a prominent barrister. The barrister recognised that Patrick's talents stretched beyond sorting the post and buying stamps. A quick discussion revealed his skill as a numbers man.

Sometime later, the lawyer was at his club, and he casually mentioned that a highly talented young man was working for him and that he feared Patrick Gallagher was too qualified for his position. The barrister had immense popularity amongst his peers, and his recommendation had been noted. Word soon travelled to the club owners, and Patrick was offered a post in the accountancy department in a flash.

He began his career at the St Regis as an accounts clerk until he had exposed a group of thieves stealing drink from the club and paying with counterfeit coins. This discovery impressed the board members, and young Patrick Gallagher's career path was set in stone. There was much debate about how much he could be trusted, after all, he was an Irishman. Ultimately, Patrick was promoted from clerk to accountant and was given some extra training to become certified. A plaque with his name on it was added to an office door. Soon, the sign was revised to say, 'head accountant'. It was a tremendous responsibility for him. Thousands of transactions were conducted each week at the club, yet Patrick never floundered or lost confidence. He was an efficient and capable man who delighted his employer.

*

The tall, dark-haired Irishman looked down at Sophie with a twinkle in his hazel-brown eyes. She was taken aback when she realised that he was looking for her.

"The postman has just been—" he said with a grin, "and there is a letter for you."

"Oh. Thank you," she muttered shyly, "Am I in trouble?"

"No, not yet," he said with a chuckle. "All the clerks are on their tea break. I was coming this way. You should be glad I intercepted it. Mrs Tremarie is infamous for opening the wrong post," Patrick said with a wink.

"Thank you, sir."

"It's my pleasure. I'm Patrick Gallagher, but you can call me Patrick," he said, with his voice deep and lilting.

It was not lost upon the Irishman that the young lady was lovely. The light strands of hair that peeped from under her cap promised a head of wild tousled red curls. Her skin was pale, and her full lips were a delicate pink. Even in the opaque steam, her blue eyes remained piercing, her gaze meeting his with confidence. For him, Sophie Bryant was soft and angelic, yet she held her head proudly. He was convinced that she wouldn't be messed with.

*

Patrick Gallagher disappeared as quickly as he had arrived. Sophie put the letter into her pocket. The other girls stared at her for a while, wondering why Patrick was playing postman to a mere laundry maid.

"Get on with it, Bryant. Move yourself. Did yer give our Paddy a feel between yer legs last night?" Amelia Holmes, Sophie's boss, crassly shouted from the back of the laundry.

Amelia Holmes had cheerful rosy cheeks and a high sweet voice, but below her soft, chubby façade lay a vindictive monster with a foul mouth.

Sophie almost died of embarrassment when she heard Amelia's accusation. The whole laundry burst into fits of laughter and whoops while Sophie had to fight back the tears of humiliation. She had forgotten about the beetroot and the pink water. All she could think of was getting away from those horrid girls and reading the letter.

*

When the bell rang to end her shift that night, she charged up the stairs and flung herself onto her thin, measly mattress.

"Aww! What's that? Have you had a letter from someone special? Who's it from?" Poppy asked with a smile.

"It looks like it's from Lady Letitia. It has the Langford stamp on it."

"Read it! Quick! Tell me everything."

Sophie ripped open the envelope and began to read. She had been correct. It was from Letitia, who wrote to ask if Sophie and Poppy were biding well in their new jobs.

"Well?"

"It says Lady Letitia has been concerned about our welfare as she hadn't heard from us. The house is quiet for lack of our mischief. She also says she's eager to remind us that our jobs await us whenever we wish to return. My parents are well. It ends by saying that she misses us and would write regularly."

When Sophie turned out her lamp at eleven twenty-nine, Poppy was full of questions, but Sophie fobbed them off. She was tired, and Lady Letitia's letter had made her homesick. She remembered that her days at Langford Manor had been happy. She didn't know how long she could tolerate the bleak environment of the club.

5

LADY MARIA GRESHAM

Lady Maria Frederica Gresham was a tall, blonde, willowy beauty with blue eyes that sparkled a deep, icy aquamarine. She was demure, sultry, and cool. Regardless of her reserved nature, she liked to make it clear that she was of Austrian blood, the same as Marie Antoinette, only luckier. Her cool façade was both enigmatic and intimidating. It was this daunting and unattainable combination that attracted men to her like moths to a flame.

All of the aristocracy had time for sport, and many gentlemen found great enjoyment in stalking innocent creatures for the pleasure of the chase, on and away from their hunting grounds. Lady Maria may have been innocent, but she was not naïve.

Before she had married, she had been considered fair game. Many a bet was placed on who would take her virginity and many a fortune lost. Young noblemen at Oxford, Cambridge and Eton had taken bets amongst each other as to who was gifted enough to lure Lady Maria out of her clothes. Try as they might, none of them had been successful. Maria was determined that she would never share her blue-blooded body with the offshoots of other, lesser, inter-bred European dynasties. She felt no awe for the mongrels who had travelled from all over Europe to finally settle on soggy little Britain.

Lady Maria's mother had been English, but her father was Austrian. She had wholly embraced her European pedigree. Maria had been raised to believe that she was more regal than the reigning British monarch.

She had lost her mother at the age of sixteen. Although she was close to her 'ma', she was relieved that her mother could no longer stubbornly force British traditions upon her. The language was crass, complex, and riddled with smatterings of German and Latin. She found the aristocratic men, clad in their stuffy tweeds, puffing at thick cigars, at best loathsome.

Lady Maria's paternal grandmother had taken responsibility for Maria's spiritual orientation at an early age. She refused that the child be raised in the Protestant faith. The child had suffered through all the milestones of Catholicism to emerge chaste and sound.

She was twenty-four when her father gave her away. There was no other way to put it. Although Maria and her grandmother were infuriated with Baron Holshausen's inhumane decision, there was no way of convincing the baron to back down. His daughter was his property, and he would trade her as he pleased. Baron Holshausen had a canny mind for business, and he knew instantly when he had met the man his daughter would marry. Holshausen was determined to thrust his virtuous daughter into the bed of the heathen, Lord Anthony George Gresham.

Maria had encountered Gresham on several occasions since. She had noted that he was handsome, charismatic, and well-educated, but all these positive characteristics had meant nothing to her because the man was not a Catholic.

When the baron gave his daughter the news of her pending nuptials, Maria was dismayed. She protested against the plan but was overruled. Her father, whom she had always adored, had betrayed her and the church. There was a giant chasm between the world of Anthony and Maria, and it was called religion.

On her wedding night, instead of celebrating, she sobbed her heart out and considered escaping to a convent.

When she voiced her devastation, Baron Holshausen had only one thing to say in his clipped Austrian accent,

> "We live in modern times, Maria. Get into his bed, give him a son, and put up with it. That is what women do."

Baron Holshausen had handpicked Lord Anthony Gresham for his daughter. The young man was very wealthy, having inherited his father's vast estate some years before. Anthony was healthy, eager, virile, and in the prime of his life. Granted, he was taking his time finding a wife, but he had decided to choose carefully. There were many women to experience on a temporary basis before he had to choose the one he could tolerate permanently. He didn't want to be saddled with a nagging bore for the rest of his life.

Anthony found neither the baron nor his beautiful daughter held any fascination for him. He thought Holshausen brash and opinionated and Lady Maria cold and abrupt. Worse, Baron Holshausen, however suave, was still perceived as a foreigner and Maria a delicate Austrian princess. Unlike medieval times, these days, the British aristocrats preferred to keep the land within a network of approved British families. Some had suggested that Lord Anthony marry his first cousin Lady Agatha. The idea was preposterous. Agatha was four years older than him, bossy, with shoulders broad enough to carry hay bales and, could bore a man to death at fifty paces.

Once Baron Holshausen knew what he wanted, he pursued Lord Anthony Gresham with a passion akin to courtship. The baron lavishly hosted Lord Anthony Gresham at Ascot. He invited the young man to numerous cultural and social events at his ostentatious Baroque home in the centre of London. Finally, he lured young Gresham to his home in the Austrian countryside. The place, in his opinion, was larger than Blenheim and far better designed.

One evening while drinking Cognac in front of the fire, the baron revealed his plan. In the most subtle fashion,

Holshausen mentioned that there was a parcel of land in Hungary that he would be delighted to buy from Lord Anthony should the occasion arise. Anthony had inherited it from an uncle he had never met and had no personal attachment to the property. European politics were complicated, allegiances were shaky, and it was mere chance that the baron had come upon the information. Gresham was not hard up for money, but Holshausen hounded the young man daily. The baron coveted the land because there were enough valuable natural resources under its rugged surface to provide a small fortune. Plus, any land en route from the landlocked Austro-Hungarian empire to towards the coveted coastline was also valuable. Everybody knew that there would be another war in Europe sooner or later. It was only a matter of time. A shrewd man would always swap war-torn land for cash. The baron was happy to play the long game.

Lady Maria gained nothing in the great arrangement. On a beautiful spring morning, she was sacrificed to the great god of greed, albeit in a Catholic cathedral. She found herself in the unpleasant but all too common position of being traded on trust, quite normal for women of her status.

Gresham had never personally considered requesting Maria's hand in marriage. In fact, he felt uncomfortable when Baron Holshausen first hinted at it. But he felt more uncomfortable at the idea of declining the offer the longer the man persisted in his pursuit. It would be a snub, a rejection, so he would have to play the game.

Holshausen paid Gresham twice the value of what the land was worth. The transaction resulted in Anthony being the wealthiest man amongst his peers. The baron was old school and unromantic. He gave Maria to Gresham like he was ridding himself of an ugly ornament at an auction. She had been traded for the best thing on offer to the baron at the time, and he was glad to be rid of her.

Before consummating their marriage, Lady Maria had explained to Anthony the gravity of the sin of marrying a Protestant like him. Not even a practising Protestant, he was dumbfounded.

> "I can't have you unhappy. What must I do to make up for this terrible sin?" Anthony asked sarcastically.

> "I don't think anything will save my soul, and my dear papa will spend until the end of time in the fires of hell."

He knew the marriage was a sham, but he never thought it would turn into a disaster quite so soon. His kind gesture of a comforting hand on her shoulder was shrugged off.

> "As you wish, but your happiness matters to me if only to keep up appearances. I will build you a private chapel here. And the local Catholic priest will visit our estate daily to say mass."

His wife thanked him for his kind gesture and then left their bedroom. It would be another week before the marriage was consummated.

Lady Maria went through the ritual at eight-o-clock every morning, irrespective of the weather. She would walk or ride to the chapel and light candles, and plead to the virgin for intervention. She genuinely feared going to purgatory, floating between this world and the next because she had married a man out of her faith. Lord Gresham brushed it off as a lot of hocus pocus and told Lady Maria as much. Her chapel and all the precious statues failed to alleviate her torment, and their union was as fractious as ever.

Anthony Gresham made peace with the rotten marriage and could tolerate it provided he didn't have to spend too much time with Maria. His wife's cool personality mirrored what lay beneath the surface of the white milky alabaster skin and finely chiselled features. For him, she was a woman as cold as the marble sculptures she prayed to.

For her, the marriage was miserable too. Lady Maria didn't care for anything but her soul, which some of her devout friends thought was admirable. But Lord Gresham found it tedious and frustrating. Maria allowed her husband access to her body once a week. Every Friday night after mass, she would undress herself and wait for him. It was always a crude, fumbled, desperate affair on his part while she lay beneath him, showing no emotion whatsoever. Anthony Gresham showed no tenderness. Instead, he got on with the job, all the time feeling angry, cheated, miserable, and resentful. He made sure that he got his one hour's worth out of her, and she lay praying all the time, partly for the Lord's forgiveness and partly that she would get pregnant and have a son and hopefully give a reprieve from his attentions. How wondrous it would be to be released of the only expectation Anthony Gresham wished her to publicly fulfil.

If Anthony had foreseen how unhappy he would be, he would have given old man Holshausen all of his Hungarian lands just to be free of the man, but it was too late now. He had married Maria under duress, and now he had a lifetime to regret it. How could he have been so stupid?

6

LORD ANTHONY GRESHAM

Lord Anthony was eagerly climbing the political ladder. He was an active user of his vote and a seat in the House of Lords. Then there was his social life, conducted as a delicate cultivating and pruning of allegiances. He had to maintain strong friendships he could call upon when needed and foster new relationships to exploit new opportunities as they presented themselves.

He didn't know why he had first chosen to pursue politics, but for all of those in the ruling class, it came with the territory of being wealthy. London was awash with politicians, activists and lobbyists.

As well as shaping the nation, there was another reason for Gresham to pursue his statesmanlike-ambitions. He explained to Maria that he found it difficult to do his work in the grand townhouse that he and his wife called home. When he told her that he was to spend most of his time living at the St Regis, he used the excuse he didn't want to disturb her with the constant stream of visitors coming to discuss this or that.

"I am sure you don't want to hear me holding court in the smoking room. It's for the best."

Maria agreed. She didn't want to be anywhere near him.

The house had the ambience of an elaborate museum that had to be kept perfect at all times, not lived in. Anthony had been raised in the country. He was quite comfortable with dog hair and faded upholstery. His mother had never needed all the pomp or the vulgar show of wealth that Maria did. Anthony constantly wondered if he should have married one of his old flames, even his burly cousin, Lady Agatha.

*

Anthony sat in his favourite comfortable, plush velvet Chesterfield. The St Regis looked over St James Square. His father had been one of the founders of the elite club. Anthony smiled to himself, wondering if the old man had also wanted to escape from his wife. He suspected he did.

Lord Jack Gresham had hated London and its modernity. He had always told Anthony that the St Regis would remain as conservative as the day that it was founded. He had insisted that there was no reason to destroy every bastion of British tradition in the name of progress and empire. The St Regis was the one place that would always be nationalist to the core. Standards could easily be maintained with one simple rule. If one was not a native Briton, you were not allowed through the stately mahogany doors.

Anthony Gresham lazed in his chair, taking in the atmosphere. The warm glow of the fires behind the brass grates reflected against the silverware. Stylish Axminster carpets softened the sound of heels walking across intricately patterned parquet and ancient marble floors. Over the years, the rich wooden wall panels had been polished with beeswax until they became a soft red-brown. The masculine aroma of Scotch, leather and tobacco combined lingered in the air without being overpowering. Billiard balls glided effortlessly across the smooth green baize after the gentle clip of a cue against an ivory ball. There was the occasional whisper of playing cards being shuffled, or from a dark corner, one would hear a discreet *'checkmate'*.

Anthony Gresham was at his home away from home. This was his domain, where he was safe from his moody wife and meddling father-in-law. As a foreigner, Baron Holshausen was only allowed as far as the dining room, which was by invitation only, and Anthony seldom invited him.

7

THE ACCIDENTAL MEETING

Daily life for the chambermaids was as onerous as those of the laundrymaids. Mrs Tremarie was a tyrannical housekeeper. She adhered to a strict timetable, and any chambermaid who didn't comply or was tardy was summoned to her office and given her marching orders forthwith. In addition, Mrs Tremarie would deny the young woman a letter of reference and go to great lengths to tarnish her name in as many social circles as she could manage. It was spiteful and unnecessarily harsh. Some of the girls joked the housekeeper would take out a full-page spread in The Times if it meant stopping the poor dismissed girl from taking a new post. She was a harsh old maid who had never married or had to care for anyone else, for that matter. Her brash judgemental nature was typical of those who had never opened their heart to love.

She had been the housekeeper at the club for twenty-five years, and her service was faultless. A dedicated member of the institution, she even lived in a small flat just off the courtyard, keeping a watchful eye on everything that took place inside and outside the building.

The board members had been emphatic upon her appointment all those years ago. The rules at the St Regis were absolute. The most important rule of all was that no women were allowed entry, but they were prepared to make an exception for housemaids. The pompous old men went on to state that they would turn a blind eye to the army of maids who invaded the club every morning at breakfast between eight-thirty and nine-thirty to infiltrate the briefly unoccupied guest rooms to dust, polish, stoke the fires, clean the toilets, and whatever else was demanded of them by the housekeeper. This type of work was far below the male staff, who served as barmen, chefs, valets, croupiers, and waiters.

Mrs Tremarie had embraced the rules with gusto and had successfully trained the chambermaids to work with precision and at twice the speed of the others in their industry. This was achieved by applying a terrifying rule of iron rather than providing the latest labour-saving devices. When the gentleman returned to his room after breakfast, he would find it clean and tidy, without a maid in sight.

Poppy had excelled in her appointment so much that she earned a rare nod from Mrs Tremarie. There had been no smile. The harpy never smiled. Poppy was efficient and punctual, two qualities the housekeeper valued highly. Poppy loved her job. Even though it was menial dirty work, there was a time-pressure attached to it, which gave it a sense of risk that appealed to her. The thought of getting a telling off from the housekeeper for bumping into a wealthy gentleman didn't seem too much of a hardship compared to Sophie scalding her forearms if she made a mistake.

There was also an entire world above stairs that few commoners had privy to. She was intrigued by which titled fellow was residing in which room. She delighted in poking about their possessions and reading their correspondence if she could get away with it. She made mental notes of who they were and what they were up to so that she could give Sophie the names later that night. It had surprised her that most suites were frugal and unfussy.

> "I can't understand why a wealthy man would rather live in the sparse confines of his club rather than the opulence of his home? Makes no sense to me, Sophie. Surely it gets dull discussing all those deals or what they read in the paper?"

*

That day, just like all the others, the routine ran as regular as clockwork. Poppy stood in the servant's corridor, waiting for Mrs Tremarie to give the signal that they could enter the club. At precisely eight-thirty, the housekeeper tapped her wristwatch, indicating they could begin. Poppy opened a discreet door that blended almost seamlessly into the wall and stepped into the cold, dull hallway of the fourth floor.

Her cart was equipped with the regular cleaning paraphernalia of a bucket, mop, broom, dusters, buffing cloths and wax polish. She wheeled the load along with the small empty tub for the slops on a hook at the front, banging against the wood.

Poppy cleaned the first rooms without any real bother. The first was reasonably clean. The second looked like a pigsty, but it was soon dealt with. Nobody had used the third.

She walked briskly to the fourth room and looked up at the door plaque. *'17'*. There was no time to dawdle. She pushed open the heavy door and pulled her cart into the large room. She was entirely focused on her task, and it was her habit to make the bed first.

As she went toward the bed, she saw the bedclothes move, and a dishevelled man sat up and looked around the room, trying to find his bearings. His dark hair was tousled, and a few strands of his fringe hung over his thick brows. He was bare to the waist. His chest and arms were well-formed, his hair short and black. There was the shadow of a beard.

Anthony Gresham fumbled for the clock on the bedside table. When he read the time, he swore. Then he looked up and saw Poppy. He felt disoriented and wondered who she was. His head felt like it was being squeezed in a vice.

"Is this my room?" he muttered.

Poppy watched dumbfounded.

"Sorry. I didn't see you," he grumbled, running his hand through his hair.

"Excuse me, sir. I will come back."

"Too much Scotch," Anthony groaned miserably.

Poppy took her cart and quickly wheeled it towards the door. She had hardly taken two steps forward when the groggy, hung over Sir Anthony Gresham threw off the blankets and climbed out of bed. He was naked. Poppy gasped as he unashamedly walked past her to the bathroom. It was the closest that Poppy had ever come to a naked man, and she was shocked, but she couldn't tear her eyes away either. His muscular form looked like an athletic Roman statue.

Anthony Gresham felt too sick to care that he was naked in front of the girl. As he walked away, he dismissively waved his hand in the air. Without looking back, he told Poppy to return the next day.

*

Poppy couldn't wait to tell Sophie what she had seen. That night she tore up the stairs to their room and thundered through the door like a battering ram.

"What's happened?" Sophie exclaimed.

Poppy put her finger to her mouth.

"Shhh!"

"What happened?" whispered Sophie.

The story tumbled out of Poppy but was steadily interrupted by Sophie, who demanded every detail. Everything was revealed by Poppy except one thing.

"Come on, Poppy! Tell me who it is!"

"I prefer to keep you guessing?"

Sophie suggested a list of names starting with the most likely, then worked on the most outrageous.

"My lips are sealed, Sophie. Stop asking. He's got dark hair. That's the only clue."

"That could be half the men who work or visit here! That's no clue, you tease!"

There was a lull in their friendly banter before Sophie made an important observation.

"What if he reports you to Mrs Tremarie, Poppy?"

"I don't think he could remember my face. We always keep the curtains closed," the bohemian girl joked.

"Oh, my goodness! You must have felt so shy."

"Truly, Sophie, I couldn't take my eyes off him," Poppy confessed.

"Don't say that!"

Sophie began to chuckle, which soon turned into a belly laugh.

"He's a man, Soph. A real man."

Poppy didn't know how to put things into words. She could never explain the desire she had felt in the brief seconds she had watched Anthony Gresham walk across the room. She had been both terrified and captivated all at once. She had felt adrenalin course through her body and found it difficult to breathe. A warm anxious feeling was squeezing her chest, and she felt it travel throughout her body.

"Do you think that he will be there again tomorrow morning?" Sophie asked.

"No, likely not. He's a busy man," Poppy sighed.

Sophie felt relieved. A brief, private dalliance with a man was perhaps acceptable with two consenting parties, but no good could come of it if it turned into a long-running affair. Hearts would definitely be broken.

"You don't understand, Sophie. He was really lovely."

"How can you say that with no shame?"

"I've never seen a real man," whispered Poppy. "But he was not like the skinny boys you see jumping in the river at summertime. He had a broad, strong chest. And his arms, well, they weren't white and wiry, they were—."

"Stop it, Poppy! Stop it. You're a maid, and don't you forget it. Just know your place."

"I think I'm in love, Sophie!"

"What? What has got into you? You've never spoken like this before."

"Sophie, it's the first time I have considered that I could love somebody so intensely. If this is how I feel just seeing him, imagine what it would be to fall in love."

"Poppy, listen to me. These men will never fall in love with the likes of us."

Such was her concern, she shook her friend by the shoulders, trying to knock some sense into her.

Poppy slumped back in her bed and looked at the ceiling. It may have been the first time that she had felt such an attraction, but also the first time she had truly resented the restriction of her class.

"I suppose you're right," Poppy said despondently.

She felt disheartened. Sophie's words had struck a chord. She knew her friend was telling the truth but resented the comment all the same. She had never really considered herself poor in the past, feeling she experienced the richness of life in other ways, but she felt incredibly poor now.

Poppy made the excuse of being tired and rolled over to face the wall. She didn't go to sleep immediately, though. Instead, she created a fantasy world in which she and Anthony Gresham were lovers. Finally, she fell into a deep sleep, dreaming of a life she could never have.

*

Poppy awoke earlier than usual and remembered the dream. She got up and dressed slowly, paying more attention to her appearance than usual. She pulled a lock of beautiful chestnut hair from under her bonnet. She rubbed her face until she saw a tinge of colour appear on her cheeks. Then, she rinsed her eyes, hoping it would encourage them to become brighter. She sprinkled a few drops of precious, delicately scented rose water on her neck and wrists, knowing it was only enough to be noticed by someone standing very close to her indeed.

*

Minutes felt like hours as Poppy stood in the servant's corridor. She fidgeted impatiently while waiting for Mrs Tremarie to give her standard signal.

Poppy decided she would clean all the rooms in her care at breakneck speed and leave Anthony Gresham's until last. She wanted to widen the slim chance that he would be there, such was her all-consuming desire to see him again.

Poppy softly turned the brass door handle to Lord Gresham's room and let herself in. The drapes were closed, making the space too gloomy to work in. She made her way towards the window and threw the heavy curtains open. The meagre light of the grey

London morning made little difference but was enough to see the shadow of a man sitting silently in the corner. Had Anthony Gresham waited for her?

Although she had hoped to encounter him again, she was still startled by his presence. Gresham stood up slowly. Poppy's senses were heightened, and she could almost feel him as he slowly walked toward her. He was wearing well-cut black trousers and no jacket. His white shirt was crisp, the collar was starched to perfection, and it contrasted against his clean-shaven jaw. His tie was off, and his top button was undone.

"Don't concern yourself with me," he said, smiling at her.

Poppy nodded.

"I sacrificed breakfast because I wanted to apologise to you."

"Yes, sir," Poppy mumbled.

"I am sorry, I don't usually parade naked in front of the maids. Please accept my apology. I was a little worse for wear after a late night."

"Yes, sir," stuttered Poppy. "No trouble at all, sir."

"I have a few things to do at my desk. Please continue as you usually do while I get on with my work."

"I am not supposed to be in a gentleman's room when he is here, sir. Mrs Tremarie will—"

"—Don't worry, you can leave that old battle axe for me to deal with if she decides to complain," he joked irreverently. "My father was a founder of this club. She knows her place when it comes to me."

Anthony Gresham could hardly make Poppy out in the haze of the morning light. He returned to his desk where he had been sitting and began reading a document. Once or twice, he lifted his head to watch the girl, studying her curvy silhouette against the light of the window.

The young maid had a beautiful profile. Even in her uniform, he noted that her body was slim yet shapely. His thoughts meandered unhelpfully to his wife and her ice-cold androgynous body. He had long since lost interest in her, and as for giving him an heir, he hoped that would happen one day, but he was starting to not care when. Until now, he had remained faithful to her, but her constant rejection drove him to fury and frustration. He was glad he no longer went home at the weekends, not missing her at all.

After a while, Anthony stood up and put his hands in his pockets while he watched Poppy polish his mirror. The girl felt self-conscious as she went about the routine of cleaning the room until the uncomfortable silence was interrupted by Gresham.

"That's enough," he ordered. "It's clean enough. I can see the future in there, never mind my face."

"Excuse me, sir?"

Anthony looked at her full sensuous mouth, white skin and soft tresses escaping from her bonnet.

"You have done a sterling job. Really. The room is clean enough now. You may leave. I need my privacy," he said abruptly.

Watching her had put him in a dark, destructive mood. The homely girl reminded him of everything that was lacking in his life. Poppy stared at him, aghast.

"Mrs Tremarie won't accept that," she answered more boldly than she intended.

"Then we won't tell Mrs Tremarie," Anthony said firmly.

"Yes, yes. Thank you, sir."

"What's your name?"

"Poppy, sir."

Poppy thought she saw him smile.

"That's a beautiful name."

Poppy left the room both terrified and elated. Anthony Gresham had apologised to her for being rude. He had sent her away without doing much work, and his lordship had even asked what her name was. This turn of events would be something to tell Sophie.

8

POLITICS

Over the years, Anthony Gresham and Patrick Gallagher had become friends. Gallagher was not of the class to be invited to dinner or a weekend in the country with his lordship, but they got along well at the club. Both men were ambitious. Anthony was driven and aggressive, while Patrick had an easy-going nature that belied his intensity. Many people had underestimated Patrick Gallagher's ambition, but they had been proven wrong.

It had become routine for Anthony and Patrick to have a drink in the guest lounge late in the evenings. They would discuss an array of subjects, from business to sports. They were so comfortable with each other that sometimes they said nothing and just sat and enjoyed the peace that accompanied the day's end.

After dinner, a satisfied hush had settled over the club, and the two men were slowly sipping their Cognac and watching the fire.

"The elections are only three months away," observed Patrick.

"I never wanted to be a politician," Anthony complained before taking a big sip of the burning amber liquid.

"There is talk that you may be appointed as an advisor to the Foreign Office Minister?"

"Yes, it's a disaster."

Patrick thought he heard a hint of bitterness in the statement.

"You can accomplish a lot of good, though, Anthony."

"I am not very good with those stuffy international ceremonies. I've had enough of those for a lifetime."

Patrick heard the resentment in Anthony's voice.

"Í would rather be with the agriculture ministry. A far more comfortable—domestic—department," Anthony grumbled. "I blame my wife for the approach by the Foreign Office. I think they are more inclined to fancy Lady Maria for a position at the dinner table than me."

"She must have impressed them. You're a lucky man," Patrick quipped good-naturedly.

"There's no luck about it. Her father is Baron Holshausen, who owns most of Austria and half of Hungary."

"Aha!" She arrived with money and influence!" Patrick exclaimed. "No wonder the Prime Minister loves you."

This time Patrick saw a flash of annoyance in Anthony's eyes.

"Yes, I sold her father the last bit of Hungary he needed for some project or other, and he gave me Maria."

"Most of your type would have been delighted. She's a bit of a looker and not short of a bob or two!"

Patrick had no airs or graces, which was what Anthony liked best about the Irishman.

"I would never have chosen her for a wife," Anthony said quietly.

"What? You're the envy of London, old bean."

"I suppose with this Foreign Office thing, I might get a distant post overseas, so I can get as far from her as possible?"

"But surely you want an heir to keep all the lovely power and influence you aristocratic types like in your family?"

"I doubt we will ever have children," Anthony said plainly.

Patrick didn't have a response. He took a sip of the Cognac and stared into the fire.

"The Austro-Hungarian Empire is becoming a powerful beast," said Gresham. "I fear the Prime Minister is hoping that my marriage to Maria can be used to strengthen ties between the two empires."

"That is an almighty task for one man, even one as ambitious as you, Anthony."

"Yes," Anthony said, nodding his head slowly. "But they must think I can do it, and so my fate is sealed."

"You can turn down their proposal?"

"That is treachery considering my relationship with my wife's family. The Holshausen family are as rich as Croesus and as powerful as Hercules. They can make life very difficult for me, even from the continent."

"But if you can pull a deal off, it will give you great power," Patrick observed.

"And eternal life with a frigid woman who won't give me children," Anthony said bitterly.

"Will not?" Patrick questioned with a confused frown?

"Will not." the lord confirmed.

They were both silent for a while.

> "My wife and I didn't consummate our marriage for a week, and things have got worse since then rather than better," conceded Anthony.

Many a man would think Anthony had already told Patrick too much, but the lord was comfortable with the confession, feeling a little bit of crushing blackness leave his soul.

The Irishman felt it best to nod, even though he was not necessarily in agreement. To date, his experiences with women had been fleeting, and he felt he could hardly offer advice.

> "There was a beautiful little thing in my room this morning," Anthony said quietly.

Patrick frowned, both confused and taken aback by Anthony's forthright manner.

> "Yes. I first saw her yesterday morning, and then she came back today."

Anthony tipped his head back to down the last of his Cognac in his glass a little bit quicker.

> "Everyone has a price, Patrick, especially impoverished young women."

Patrick frowned and became unresponsive, preferring to stare into the fire. Anthony Gresham knew that he had gone a step too far with the unburdening. Then he had to know.

"This girl, you're not going to put a price on her head, are you?"

"Ah, you worry too much, Irishman," said Anthony cheerily. "Every so often, I forget where you came from."

Lord Gresham placed his empty glass on the side table and stood up on wobbly legs.

"To bed, to bed," he said with a smile. "I will dream of the lovely Poppy all night long until she awakens me in the morning."

The aristocrat left Patrick looking shocked before he staggered off towards the corridor that led to the fourth floor. He stopped here and there to say a slurred good night to other patrons and then climbed the stairs to his room.

Patrick Gallagher stayed in the lounge and stared into the fire for a long time. He didn't touch his Cognac again and was oblivious to the room slowly emptying.

He knew the girl that Anthony was talking about. He had noticed she and Sophie were friends and shared a room. It didn't sit well with Patrick that Gresham was paying so much attention to a maid. Anthony was usually a good bloke, but hinting at his unsavoury intentions was a worry.

Patrick didn't like the idea of Lord Anthony Gresham seducing a young woman because he had marital problems, and she was poor and desperate. It reminded him of his mother's predicament all those years ago.

Patrick Gallagher had never had reason to question Anthony Gresham's integrity. Until now. From Gresham's perspective, this seemingly innocuous conversation would cause the first crack in one of his most important relationships.

9

MR ALDRIDGE

Sophie was furious at herself. By accident, she had set down a red hot cauldron upon Mr Gallagher's shirt and burned the sleeve. The iron handles on the pot were so hot that her hands had begun to burn, and instead of dropping it onto the floor and risking hurting someone else, she instinctively put it on the table next to her. The dark singe was as clear as day. The instant she saw it, she knew she would have to forfeit her day off. Worse still, her wages would be docked to cover the damage. Escaping the place would now be another seven days away or more.

Amelia Holmes, the fat old nag, took great pleasure in announcing to the entire laundry that Sophie Bryant had been lazy and irresponsible. She also took the opportunity to use her as an example of what happened when girls made mistakes, delighting in dishing out public humiliations.

"My hands were getting burned," Sophie retaliated.

"Then, you should have put it on the floor and not ruined a perfectly good shirt belonging to a fine gentleman."

"If I had dropped it, it would have splashed all over me—or someone else. Whoever the boiling water landed on would have been burnt raw!" protested Sophie.

"Your blistered legs would be the least of my worries. Now I must explain to Mr Gallagher that his shirt is destroyed, and by whom."

Sophie was about to respond, but Miss Holmes interrupted her.

"No more cheek from you, Bryant. I have a good mind to show you the door as it is. Unless you're going to offer yourself to him again to save your job to stave off a trudge to the workhouse?" she cackled cruelly.

Some of the other women cracked up with laughter. Those who had already experienced Miss Holmes foul mouth went about their work silently.

Sophie was overcome with wrath. She felt the same as she had the day that her father had wanted to whip her for losing her temper with Freddy McMillin. She would have left without a second thought, but she had nowhere to safe go. She decided to seek another temporary position as soon as she could take leave, then think about making her way back to Longford Manor, and after that, think about how to rescue Poppy.

It had been a long day, and at eleven that night, Sophie finished up at her station and slowly climbed the steps to her room, exhausted and despondent. She had been so looking forward to her day off. All she wanted to do was walk outside, even if it was pouring with rain. Now she had gone and spoilt it all for herself because she had made a stupid mistake. She went to her room, hoping to find a friendly ear to confide in, but instead, she found herself fuming. There was her friend, lying on the bed, smiling as if she was the cat that got the cream.

Poppy didn't wait for Sophie to close the door before she began bombarding her with her day's thrilling details.

"Sophie, I have so much to tell you!"

"Not tonight, Poppy. I just want to sleep and forget the day."

"Listen to me," Poppy insisted in a stage whisper, "Lord Gresham spoke to me this morning. He asked my name."

"Tell me tomorrow."

Sophie put on her nightdress and climbed under the scratchy thin bedclothes.

"He said it was a lovely name, so he did."

Sophie ignored her.

"What's got into you then, Lady Muck?"

"I've had a right day, and I don't want to listen to your incessant childish ramblings about Lord Gresham."

"You're just jealous, Sophie Bryant. You're jealous that a man like Lord Gresham can look at me and talk to me."

"Far from it. I have had a terrible day. My pay is docked, and I've lost my day off!"

Instead of solace, Sophie got another rebuke.

"Quieten down. You are making a right old racket. Old Tremarie will come in here any moment now, and you will be in worse trouble!"

Sophie was in no mood to be tamed.

"This is a miserable hole, and you got me into a great mess by bringing me here. I should have known better. You said we could go home if it was horrid here, and it is. When are we leaving? We agreed to go together, and it's been weeks."

"I am not sure," Poppy stammered.

"You promised."

"Things have changed."

"Apart from getting worse, how so?" demanded Sophie.

"Oh, sweetheart, I am so sorry about your pay and your day off. If I had known, I wouldn't have attacked you with my good news. But you have to hear what happened to me. Lord Gresham—"

Sophie had heard enough. *'Stupid, stupid, Poppy.'*

The young girl couldn't suppress her feelings any longer. She'd had enough of Mrs Tremarie, Amelia Holmes, and now she had enough of her friend.

"Poppy, your obsession with Lord Gresham will just lead to trouble, and I don't want to be your friend when it happens."

"What do you mean by that?"

"Go to sleep. I've had enough of you for today."

Poppy pestered Sophie, but she pulled her head under her covers and ignored her. She decided that Sophie was jealous because someone else had made her happy. A man had made her happy.

Sophie was tired of Poppy's constant wheeling and dealing to get her own way. So, what if Lord Gresham had noticed her? She had probably flaunted herself in front of him like a common tart.

Looking at her friend's frosty back facing towards her, for the briefest moment, Poppy allowed herself to remember that Anthony Gresham was married. She swept the thought out of her mind as fast as it had arrived. It was no time to complicate her fantasies by thinking about adultery and its dire consequences.

It took a while for Sophie to fall asleep, and when she did, her sleep was punctuated with chaotic dreams of unrecognisable images whirling in a great grey mist. It was not a terrifying dream, but she awoke in the morning feeling more exhausted than the night before.

*

Patrick opened the note on his desk informing him that his shirt sleeve had been burned while in the laundry. He crumpled the letter and threw it into the wastepaper basket underneath his desk, unaffected by the news. The shirt was old, and he needed to replace it anyway.

It was Friday afternoon, and Patrick was mulling over the wage register, checking that Mr Aldridge had calculated the columns correctly and that nothing had been omitted. Patrick was always appalled at how little the staff were paid. It embarrassed him that people worked twice as hard as he did and were paid so poorly. The adverts always stated a good wage, but after all the stoppages and extras, it was a pittance. Every Friday afternoon, he was riddled with guilt when he looked at the figures that Mr Aldridge presented.

Patrick had once commented to Anthony that the club could have tripled the staff's wages and still run at a hefty profit.

> "Stop feeling guilty, Irishman," Anthony replied. "Not everyone has a valuable skill. All they are capable of is cleaning and serving. Under the circumstances, they are lucky to have work at all."

Patrick was irritated with Anthony's flippant reply.

"Would you clean and cook for yourself?"

Lord Anthony looked at him aghast.

"Never, I wouldn't know where to begin cooking a roast turkey," he chuckled.

"And your commode?"

"You're right, Irishman. Thank God for servants and plumbing."

Patrick Gallagher wanted to drive the point home. It was an ugly side to his friend's otherwise agreeable personality.

"I believe that servants should be paid as well as any artisan is. More so, if it's a terrible job, then they should be paid much more to ensure they keep making life easier for the wealthy."

Anthony sat upright in his chair, finally realising he knew that he was being challenged.

"The poor are vultures eating of the flesh of the rich, Patrick. The wretches would only want more if we paid a better wage."

"How much would you charge to clean a lavvy?"

"At least a thousand pounds," laughed the aristocrat.

"Now, do you see my point, Anthony? The going rate for getting a lavvy, sparklingly clean should be one thousand pounds, or you can do it yourself."

"Never!"

"Have you ever collected the slops and carried a foetid bucket down four flights of stairs. Have you ever seen and smelt it when you pour it out?"

"Thankfully, I don't need to," sighed Anthony.

"Well, perhaps you should be more grateful someone is prepared to do it for you instead of fleecing them!"

The lord stared at the wily Irishman. Patrick Gallagher had put forward a sound argument, and he had to concede that he enjoyed his creature comforts. He had no intentions of polishing his own shoes or raking up horse dung in his courtyard at home.

Patrick observed Lord Anthony's reaction and judged it well.

"I am saying that you may need to compensate people fairly, or you'll have to do the work yourself. Our rate of churn of staff is pitiful. I can't say I blame them if they get a better offer."

Anthony Gresham stared at Patrick Gallagher from under his brow.

> "I am watching you, Irishman," Lord Anthony said, feeling slightly unsettled but managing a false chuckle. "You're a dark horse. Like one of those union men protesting at Trafalgar Square at times, aren't you? Must have been your years by docks at Salford."

Patrick wanted to mention the sacrifices his mother had endured to make sufficient money to send him to school, but he stopped short. He realised that he was becoming angry and that it would never alter the past, alleviate his guilt over her sacrifice, or change his friend's outlook.

Gallagher had to get away. He had excused himself with a ready smile and the excuse that he had work to do.

*

Patrick signed the bottom of the page, thus approving Mr Aldridge's work and then handed the books back to the wage clerk.

> "Thank you, Mr Aldridge. That all balances. Please make up the pay packets ready to give to the staff on Saturday night after supper."

*

Simeon Aldridge sat at the large refectory table in the kitchen. A tin box was set down at his elbow. He dug in his pocket and produced a little brass key that unlocked the box. Inside was the paltry amount of money that he had to dish out. Mr Aldridge was an elderly man, tall, bald and had a slight paunch. His defining feature was his spectacles balanced precariously at the bottom of his long Roman nose. Mr Aldridge was a kind man who harboured great empathy for those less fortunate than he was.

Each Saturday evening, the staff stood in a long queue waiting for their turn to be paid. Mr Aldridge had worked at the club for an eternity and prized himself for knowing every person in the building by name.

He greeted them all in a friendly fashion, answered their questions respectfully and treated everybody with dignity. Aldridge was the epitome of a middle-class gentleman.

He always breathed a sigh of relief when he had paid the last person in the line. Finally, he could go home to his family. As he closed the money box, he was surprised to find it didn't close properly. One envelope remained, almost invisible, crunched up behind the front edge of the box. He knew that he had not made a mistake. He never made mistakes. But someone else had.

He took out the giant ledger and began searching the columns for a name that didn't have a mark for the date in question. When he reached Sophie Bryant's name, there was no signature or cross to signify that she had received her pay.

Mr Aldridge called for Old Amelia, who was pacing around the laundry room, looking for something to complain about on Monday. She saw the burnt shirt sleeve, and an evil smile shaped her fat face.

"Miss Holmes, please call Miss Bryant. She has not collected her wages."

"Ah, yes, sir. Sophie Bryant is ill. Give it to me then. I will make sure that she gets it."

"That is so kind of you, ma'am, very thoughtful indeed. My legs aren't up to all those stairs. Besides, I don't think the girls would appreciate me wandering around their dormitory!"

Miss Holmes slid the little envelope into her pocket.

"Make sure you pop your initials in the ledger so we know who collected the money."

"Yes, Mr Aldridge. You'd better be getting yourself off now. I'll take the book back in the morning."

Now it was Aldridge's turn to make a mistake. He had taken it for granted that the woman was being kind. Yet, somehow, something didn't seem to add up in his beancounter mind. Simeon pushed the thought to the back of his mind. At least two girls were always too sick to fetch their money on a Saturday evening, and Miss Holmes always collected on their behalf. The girls had never complained.

It was getting late. He grabbed his hat and coat, keen to get home as soon as possible to celebrate what was left of his wife's birthday.

He called *'cheerio'* over his shoulder and disappeared into the courtyard. He left by the servant's entrance, and the moment he felt the icy London air on his face, he walked quickly to St James' Square, where he hailed a cab. All thoughts of Sophie Bryant, Miss Holmes and work, were forgotten.

10

MISS HOLMES

Monday morning dawned dull and sad. A heavy atmosphere hung over the laundry room. Miss Holmes had spent her whole Sunday dreaming up ways to further torment Sophie. There was no end to her spite.

"Bryant, get here," she heard Miss Holmes bellow.

Sophie made her way over to the old spinster, waiting for her with one fat hand on her immense hip and the damaged shirt in the other.

> "Get this up to Mr Gallagher. Tell him it's all your fault that it's damaged beyond recognition," Holmes exaggerated before throwing the garment at her.

Sophie caught it. Miss Holmes had docked her pay, made her forfeit her day off, and now she had to face Patrick Gallagher and explain why he needed a new shirt.

She straightened her back, lifted her head proudly, and walked past Miss Holmes without a word. The old crone had gone a step too far this time, and Sophie would show no fear. She was not going to feed another monster who seemed to delight in tormenting her.

Sophie took the servant's staircase to Patrick Gallagher's office. She'd never been in that part of the building before, and it was refreshing to be out of the laundry rooms.

Sophie went into the main office where all the clerks sat. It was a grey room full of grey people. The only person who showed anything bright was Mr Aldridge, with his burgundy handkerchief peeping out of his top pocket.

"Ah, good day, Miss Bryant," he chirped.

"Hello, Mr Aldridge," Sophie gazed about the room taking in everything.

"They are all rather grey, aren't they?" Mr Aldridge whispered.

Sophie smiled.

"They seem to wear the weather when they come to work. Try as I may, they refuse to brighten up, fearing they may look garish."

Sophie chuckled.

"How are you feeling, my dear? I believe that you were ill."

"Me?" Sophie asked. "But, I've not been ill?"

"How strange, Miss Holmes told me you were a little out of sorts on Saturday."

"Not at all. I have nothing wrong with me, now or then. I'm in fine fettle, I promise."

"Oh, ignore me. I can be a silly old fool at times."

Mr Aldridge looked at the shirt in her hand.

"What's that?" he asked politely.

"Miss Holmes says I need to hand it to Mr Gallagher personally," Sophie explained.

"Did she," he mused, staring at the burn mark, his wheels ticking. "Well, let me show you to his office."

Patrick's office was an overcrowded shamble of books and files. When anyone mentioned the state of the room, he told them that he knew where everything was and didn't dare change a thing. Mr Aldridge knocked gently and then pushed at the door.

"Ah, Miss Bryant."

Patrick's smile was broad and sincere.

"Good morning," Sophie greeted nervously. "I'm returning your shirt. I'm afraid I damaged it. Miss Holmes asked me to give it to you personally and apologise for my carelessness."

"Really? Miss Holmes has already sent me a note to explain, and I told her to discard it. I am surprised to see that tatty old thing has been returned," he said with a frown. "I only wear it when I'm stuck in that dusty old storeroom doing a stock check. I use it to cover up my nice shirt underneath."

"I am sorry about the damage, Mr Gallagher. Miss Holmes docked my pay, and I lost my day off to teach me a lesson. I am certain I won't make the same mistake again."

Sophie smiled weakly.

Patrick Gallagher's frown lines deepened. The penalty for ruining something he thought was already fit for the bin seemed unduly severe. Patrick took the shirt from her, crumpled it into a ball and threw it into the wastepaper basket. Sophie looked bemused. Why was she in so much trouble with Miss Holmes if Patrick wasn't angry about the fate of his old shirt?

"Miss Bryant, we are human, and we make mistakes. Trust me when I say that I don't hold you accountable."

"Thank you, sir."

"When is your next day off?"

"In a month, sir."

"Let's change that in the rota, shall we? I shall tell Miss Holmes that you will be rescheduling your day off, not losing it. And let us make an appointment to have tea."

"Yes, sir. Thank you, sir!"

"I shall speak to Miss Holmes and Mrs Tremarie. I want to make it up to you for causing this sorry mess. I should have rinsed my old shirt, taken it with me, and not left it on the table."

"But!"

"No buts, Miss Bryant."

Sophie was taken aback, worried his kind gesture might lead to even more humiliations from the senior staff when he wasn't looking.

"Just knowing you are not angry with me for my blunder is recompense enough."

"I insist."

Patrick Gallagher was adamant. Sophie stood with her mouth open as she watched the Irishman summon his assistant back into the room.

"Mr Aldridge, this business with my old shirt has cost Miss Bryant her week's wages and her day off. I mean to make it up to her, please diarise the second Sunday in September. I will be taking her out for tea."

Mr Aldridge smiled. He was fiercely proud of Patrick Gallagher's good heart.

"What a wonderful idea," Simeon agreed. "That reminds me. About the wages, Mr Gallagher. There's something we need to discuss."

"Fine. Please close the door on your way out, Miss Bryant."

Sophie went back to the laundry, pleased that she had been brave enough to face the Irishman, pleased that he had taken it so well, and very pleased that Patrick had offered to take her out for tea on her next day off. It was the first kind gesture she had experienced in weeks. She wouldn't have enough time and money to return to Longford, but at least she would have a reprieve from the oppressive atmosphere in the club.

Miss Holmes was disappointed when she saw Sophie return. The humble girl looked calm and unperturbed. It was not what the horrible woman had intended, and she flung a pail across the room in anger. She had hated Sophie from the day she had watched Patrick Gallagher hand deliver Lady Longford's letter to her. She had seen how the man had looked at her. In Amelia's mind's eye, Sophie Bryant thought she was better than everybody else, and she needed bringing down a peg or two.

*

Lord Gresham had opened a floodgate when he had admitted to Patrick Gallagher and quite a few other club members that he found Poppy provocative. It seemed having a relationship with a maid was not as unthinkable as it sounded. Many of his peers eradicated bouts of boredom by pursuing physical relationships with their staff. It was not uncommon for servants of both genders to please their masters. Some men even said how cost-effective a pleasure it was. Very little passed between master and servant except gaining favour and their underlings having an extra afternoon off on a quiet day.

Few wives acknowledged that their husbands strayed. Most welcomed a hiatus from their husbands' incessant physical demands. Others were humiliated but kept it to themselves, not wanting to be pitied.

Lord Gresham knew that Lady Maria would be neither relieved nor humiliated. She would make the most of the pity and use other people's moral compasses to provide the opportunity to leave with her wifely reputation intact. She didn't believe in divorce and would never seek an annulment from the pope. Lady Maria would ensure she was seen as the *'injured party'* and simply go and live in Austria.

If Anthony Gresham had been in this situation with a little minx six months earlier, he would have been delighted. Unfortunately, now he had been coaxed into politics, he had been parachuted into the midst of London society, where everyone was interested in everyone else's dark secrets.

Contrary to his initial expectations, he had been enjoying the challenge of political debate and the satisfaction of outwitting his opponents. For the first time in many years, he felt alive and respected. He was slowly beginning to understand the benefits of being powerful. As much joy as his rebirth gave him, he knew that his wife, Lady Maria Holshausen Gresham, was integral to his success. But if anyone found out about a dalliance with Poppy, that could all come crashing down.

Anthony had seen many a good man destroyed because of the slightest of indiscretions. He would need to be very, very careful.

*

Poppy's heart was beating so fast that she thought it would explode out of her chest. She had saved Lord Anthony Gresham's room for last again. She knew in her marrow that as sure as the sun rose in the east, he would be there waiting for her.

She let herself into his room and quickly shut the door behind her. The curtains were drawn, and she could barely see her palm before her face, but she sensed his presence.

"Good morning," came his deep voice coming from the bed.

"Good morning, sir," Poppy answered breathlessly.

Anthony Gresham got out of bed and walked toward her. Only when he was right beside her did she realise he was naked. He reached out and gently removed her bonnet. Ever so gently, he removed the pins from her hair until her curls hung down her back and around her face.

Anthony Gresham undid the two top buttons of her bodice, and then he stopped.

"I can't do this to you," he said gruffly.

Poppy wanted to cry. She had been so confident that he would want her.

"I am sorry," she said, embarrassed.

He took her face and turned it toward him.

"There is no need to be sorry," he purred. "You have done nothing wrong."

Poppy twisted her hair into a knot and shoved it under her bonnet, desperate to escape.

"I am terrified that I will fall in love with you," the calculating Gresham blurted out.

He was so close to her, but she was too scared to reach out and touch him. He smelled the delicate scent of rosewater, a sign she wanted to impress him. Her heart lurched when he said the words, and his vulnerability almost broke her heart.

"Do you know that I am a married man?" he whispered before adding, "Unhappily married."

Sophie nodded in the dark.

"My wife is a miserable woman. I need someone to love me and treat me with tenderness."

Sophie put her hand out and ran it down his chest.

"I can look after you," she stuttered softly, shocked by her quick confession.

"I must see you tonight. I can't bear the loneliness anymore."

He sounded heartbroken.

"I need physical love. I was taken by your beauty when I watched you the other morning. You left me mesmerised, and I couldn't work all day. I was tossing and turning all night. I couldn't get you out of my mind. Come to me tonight. Nobody will know. I will make sure of it."

The wide-eyed and innocent Sophie nodded, no longer playing the role of the wild, worldly girl who loved acting up.

"Can I trust you to keep our secret?"

"Yes," whispered Poppy.

Lord Anthony Gresham leaned forward and kissed her, gently at first, then with more insistence. He held her against his naked body. The embrace was sensual, and it stirred something deep inside the girl.

"I don't want you to leave," he mumbled in a desperate tone as if he was in pain.

"I have to go," Poppy begged reluctantly, trying to wriggle free from his passionate grip. "Mrs Tremarie will realise that I am missing."

Poppy turned around and ran toward the door pulling the cart behind her. Mrs Tremarie tapped her watch and raised her eyebrows when she saw Poppy come out of Lord Gresham's room.

"You're becoming slack, Miss Patterson," the housekeeper chastised.

"I am sorry, Mrs Tremarie. All the rooms were in a shocking state this morning. I swear I went as fast as I could!"

"See you don't let it happen again."

"No, Mrs Tremarie"

*

Anthony Gresham smiled as he watched Poppy leave the room. He was satisfied with his achievement. Women would do anything for a man who feigned he was in love with them. It worked every time. He got dressed and made his way to the breakfast room, where he saw Patrick Gallagher.

"Good morning, Irishman," he said, smiling broadly.

"What has put you in such a good mood on this grey wintry day?"

"Ah, wouldn't you like to know?"

Patrick felt his temper flare. He knew precisely what Lord Anthony Gresham meant, and it made him sick to the stomach. He wouldn't be able to eat breakfast at the same table as the man.

"Sorry, your lordship," Patrick said abruptly. "I have work to do."

Patrick turned on his heel and walked away. Anthony Gresham was too self-important to realise that Patrick Gallagher was appalled by his behaviour. Patrick couldn't understand what had happened to the fellow who was once his friend. It was like the man had been possessed by a demon. The cracks in their relationship, like the ones between the lord and his wife, were also becoming a chasm.

*

After Sophie Bryant left the office, Simeon went and stood in front of a large bookcase. The old man was meticulous. He reached for the giant ledger, where he recorded the week's wages and where the staff signed to confirm that they had received the correct amount. Many of the servants could recognise numbers but were otherwise illiterate. The columns were littered with crosses. Next to each cross, Mr Aldridge had carefully written the name of the person who had received the money directly or by designated proxy. His set of books went back years. The clerk could produce more than a decade of information at the drop of a hat.

Mr Aldridge was delighted. He had a puzzle to solve. Sophie Bryant had said that her pay had been docked because she had burnt Patrick's shirt, yet he remembered Miss Holmes saying that Sophie was ill and would take her wages and deliver them. He recalled watching Amelia slip the little envelope into her pocket. When he looked at the figures, almost every week, it appeared Miss Holmes would collect money under the auspices of one or two of her girls, being too ill to fetch it themselves.

Mr Aldridge began to study the columns earnestly. He worked his way back methodically and made a list of all the laundry maids who had been too sick to collect their pay. Next to each name, rather than a cross, there was a neatly written insert, *'AH'*. Then, he began to calculate the amount of money the old laundress had collected on behalf of her staff. The total was staggering. Over the last two years, Miss Holmes had collected several hundred pounds. Mr Aldridge was astounded. If this is what she had stolen in two years, he wondered how much she had stolen over the entire ten that she had worked at the club.

Mr Aldridge sat back in his chair and rhythmically tapped his pencil on his desk. He was deep in thought. He would do a thorough investigation and take the results to Patrick Gallagher. The potential problem he had alluded to after Sophie's revelation was not a figment of his imagination.

11

THE INVITATION

Poppy dared not share her secret with Sophie. Lord Gresham had begged her to be discreet, and she had promised that she would be loyal to him. Besides, Sophie would never approve, and the last thing Poppy needed was someone else whinging at her. Mrs Tremarie's potential for unleashing her disdain seemed limitless. The girl spent the day dwelling upon what her beau had told her.

Poppy thought that Sophie would never fall asleep, and it was after midnight when she quietly slipped into the servant's corridor and then entered the hallway that led to Gresham's room. She stroked her fingernails softly against the door marked *'17'*.

He greeted her, fully clothed and full of impatience.

"I didn't think you would come. I thought you had become frightened."

Poppy shook her head.

"I was only afraid that someone may see me."

Anthony moved toward Poppy. When he reached her, he cupped her face in his hands. He did it tenderly, reeling her in like an expert fisherman. He wanted to enjoy every moment of seducing the innocent young woman. The thought of it being her first time added to his arousal. He tilted her head toward him and kissed her, stroking the nape of her neck, then sliding his hands down to the small of her back. He led her to his bed and slowly undressed them both. He relished in the pleasure of feeling her body against his. It was good to have a woman who desired him. He had satisfied his frustration with an array of women, but Poppy was different. He was her first lover, and she wasn't an experienced woman who had seen most of London naked. He could teach poor naïve Poppy all the fine arts of lovemaking that most polite women discouraged.

That night, Lord Anthony Gresham took full advantage of Poppy Patterson.

*

Afterwards, he held her in his arms and told her all the lies that she wanted to hear.

"Promise me that you will never leave me," he whispered as he caressed her cheek.

"I promise, sir."

"Call me Anthony, please, sweetheart. Look, I know it's so soon, but—"

"—Go on—"

"I love you, Poppy. I have waited for someone like you my entire life."

"I feel the same," Poppy answered shyly.

Ever the gentleman, the lord helped his latest conquest back into her clothes.

"You must hurry back to your quarters," he insisted. "Nobody must know that you are missing. If someone finds out, it will make it impossible for me to see you again. I couldn't bear that."

"When will I see you again, my love?" Poppy asked.

"Do you want to be with me every night?" Anthony asked, pretending to be concerned.

"Yes," Poppy answered truthfully. "I never want us to be apart."

He opened the door for the girl and watched her tip-toe down the hall. She slipped through the hidden door and out into the service corridor.

Still wide awake, Sophie heard her friend open the door and climb into bed. She wondered where the girl had been, but she was too exhausted to string her thoughts together properly. She decided everything was above board and that Poppy must have gone to the washrooms before dozing off into a deep, peaceful sleep.

The following day the laundry room was chaotic. There had been a rowdy banquet the night before, and the table linens were in a terrible state. It was midday before she remembered Poppy's late-night escapade. Since the girl had mentioned nothing about it, Sophie decided that what she didn't know couldn't harm her.

*

It took a few hours, but a delighted Simeon Aldridge had finally assimilated all the facts and figures concerning Miss Holmes' pilfering. He put a summary of all the evidence in a neat pile, popped slivers of paper in the ledger to bookmark every transgression, and then asked Patrick Gallagher for a second meeting.

He went into Patrick's office and shut the door behind him.

"It must be a serious matter if you insist on shutting the door," Patrick said with a laugh.

"Indeed, it is." The clerk answered solemnly.

"Come on, it can't be that serious, can it?" Patrick sniggered.

"Unfortunately, it's no laughing matter, Mr Gallagher. I am afraid one of our employees is guilty of defrauding her colleagues."

"Who?"

"Miss Holmes, the head laundress."

"That grouchy old spinster, who lives here rent-free?"

"Yes," answered Mr Aldridge.

"Explain it to me, Simeon. Why would a single woman with no real overheads need to steal from us?"

Patrick looked at the pile of documents that Mr Aldridge started transferring to his desk and then sighed.

"By the looks of it, she did a pretty good job of it over a long period."

"Unfortunately, yes," admitted Aldridge. "All the girls were too scared to complain about her, so we never knew what was happening. We would never have caught her if young Sophie Bryant had not burnt your shirt."

Mr Aldridge spent an hour explaining to Patrick how easily Miss Holmes had embezzled money from the laundry staff under his very nose. He traced his finger down column upon column of figures. At the end of his speech, he disclosed the amount that she had stolen.

Patrick whistled softly at the eye-watering amount and stared at Mr Aldridge in disbelief.

"Do you think Mrs Tremarie knew this was happening?"

"I very much doubt it," answered Mr Aldridge. "The girls who work in the laundry are terrified of Amelia Holmes. She curses and degrades them all day. She is a bully, and she encourages the older women to intimidate the younger ones. Although I have no proof, I suspect they might be in on it."

"Why are we only learning about this now?" Patrick said, looking very unimpressed.

"I began interviewing the young ladies in confidence as soon as I realised that something was awry. After that, the truth came tumbling out one girl at a time. I am sorry, Patrick. I should have noticed the inconsistencies a long time ago."

"Not to worry, Mr Aldridge. We are right to trust our staff in good faith. An honest man will always find it difficult to notice or accept that his peers may be sly."

Patrick realised what he had said, and for a few moments, he was distracted by the crossed words he had had with Anthony earlier. He used to trust the man to be ethical, but now he had to accept that the man was making a name for himself in political circles, and he was becoming ever more cunning and manipulative. He felt the pain of disappointment more than anger. He was saddened that Anthony Gresham had fooled him and upset that he had turned a blind eye at times and let it happen.

"Mr Aldridge, please arrange a meeting with Miss Holmes, Mrs Tremarie and Jones, the butler."

*

The following morning Sophie was summoned to a meeting in Mrs Tremarie's office. She was surprised when she saw who all were in attendance.

"Don't be afraid, Sophie," said Mr Aldridge, " we have testimony from many girls. It's just that your case is the most recent."

Sophie looked like a petrified rabbit, frozen in the instant it decided if it wanted to run and hide.

"It's a simple question I'd like you to answer truthfully."

Sophie gulped.

"We'd like you to tell us if you received your wages from Miss Holmes last week."

Amelia glared at the girl, but it was too late. Sophie's wild, renegade streak was front and centre once more.

"No. I did not receive my wages. And I had to forfeit my day off."

Simeon read out a note he had shared with all the girls who had probably been defrauded, followed by the list of names beneath with 'x's scribbled next to them.

"I also have some written statements from all those girls who could manage it."

He dropped a pile of notes on a spike onto Patrick's desk.

Gallagher skim read a few, sighing and rubbing his head. The young Irishman was outraged.

"The scale of the victimisation, abuse and even blackmail. Well, it's appalling, Mr Aldridge."

"Did you know about this?" he demanded of the housekeeper and the butler.

Mrs Tremarie and the butler looked at each other sheepishly. They had never expected the young Irish upstart to haul old lags like them over the coals. How dare he?

"I have a good mind to fire the sorry lot of you,".

"Now, that won't be necessary, Mr Gallagher," Tremarie said, trying to appease him. "I assure you that I will take care of this."

"You have not taken care of it to date, Mrs Tremarie. I refuse to believe you will do it now," Patrick said firmly.

"It does seem a lot of fuss for such a paltry sum. What's a few pack packets here and there? Miss Holmes can repay it to put an end to the matter. We can't just dismiss her. She is an integral part of the machinery below stairs."

"I am afraid it's more serious than a few shillings, Mrs Tremarie," Patrick said through gritted teeth.

"Mr Aldridge, please give us the total of what Miss Holmes has embezzled over the last ten years."

"One thousand, three hundred and twenty-seven pounds, thirty-two pence."

Mrs Tremarie slumped in her chair, and Mr Jones gasped. Sophie watched on agog as chaos ensued. Miss Holmes jumped to her feet, her jowls jiggling as she yelled and spat out curses and insults.

"I will get you, Sophie Bryant. I will make you pay for this, you little tart. You and Patrick Gallagher are having a good old romp, so you are. That is why you are getting away with this."

Patrick could have strangled the woman for her lewd suggestion. But, instead, he looked at Simeon.

"Mr Aldridge, please ensure that every girl who's been cheated is paid in full. Even if we have to trace them to another country. Mrs Tremarie, every young lady who has had to forfeit a day will get to take this whole weekend off."

Mrs Tremarie jumped to her feet.

"This is outrageous. We will never cope."

"I suggest you find a way. As for you, Miss Holmes, the police are outside. You will be arrested. I suspect the magistrate is going to take a rather dim view of what you've been up to."

Miss Holmes didn't know when to stop. She embarked upon another tirade, cursed everyone in the room, and threatened them with their lives. Finally, she made a desperate dive at Sophie, but Patrick stopped her.

Sophie could hear many pairs of hobnailed-boots on the chequered marble tiles. The shouting had become too much for the inquisitive investigating officer. Patrick opened the door to the officers, who promptly arrested Miss Holmes.

Sophie was soon the heroine of the laundry, and the young women who worked with her were delighted when they heard that the evil Amelia had got her just deserts. However, those closest to the criminal laundress held their mouths, fearing they would be next. They would never find work if they had a reputation for being thieves.

By eleven o'clock that night, Sophie was exhausted. There had been far too much excitement for one day.

As she passed the housekeeper's open office, Mrs Tremarie wanted to reprimand her but resisted. She would have loved to have told Sophie Bryant the consequences for making her look unprofessional and inept. She had dedicated her life to the St Regis Club, and now she looked like a fool. The board would discipline her harshly for her blunder. How dare the little upstart pull the rug from under her. Sophie Bryant would have her comeuppance.

The housekeeper got up, stuck her head into the corridor, and called out Sophie's name.

"Mr Aldridge delivered this note for you," she said, holding out an envelope to Sophie.

"Thank you."

"Are you going to open it?"

Mrs Tremarie couldn't control her curiosity.

"No," answered Sophie, making no attempt to explain herself.

"Oh yes, I forgot that you can't read. Perhaps I can help you."

Mrs Tremarie was snide and desperate.

"There's no need. I can read, Mrs Tremarie. I just refuse to read in front of you."

Mrs Tremarie realised that she had lost some of her power and she would never be respected in the same manner as before.

*

Sophie climbed the staircase to her room. All she wanted to do was sleep. But, when she was behind closed doors, she tore open the letter expecting it to be formal. Instead, it was a note from Patrick Gallagher:

Dear Miss Bryant,

Please join me for tea at the Lyon's Tearooms, Piccadilly, at three o'clock on Saturday afternoon.

Yours sincerely

Mr P Gallagher, Esq.

Sophie smiled. She slipped the letter under her pillow, then put her head down and fell asleep in minutes.

12

THE LYON'S TEAROOMS PICCADILLY

Sophie stood over the road from the tearoom, trying to will herself off the pavement and to cross the street. She was in a posh part of the city, or at least she thought so. The people and buildings looked intimidating, and she felt out of place. She even passed a massive cream-and-maroon-coloured tram that she'd never seen before. The second-hand dress she'd found at the market looked beautiful when she first put it on. Now, compared to the women around her, she felt cheap and dowdy, just like she did in Trafalgar Square when she first arrived. Sophie didn't realise that she could have worn a flour sack, and she would still have been the most beautiful girl in the room for Patrick Gallagher.

Waiting outside, Sophie was ten minutes early. Considering she couldn't pluck up the courage to walk across the road or go into the Grand Tea Emporium, it was impressive that at least she made it close to the rendezvous on time. Then, she heard a lilting voice behind her at five minutes to three.

"Good day, Miss Bryant. Shall I help you to cross the road?"

It was the jovial voice of Mr Gallagher. Without giving it a second thought, he took her hand, tucked it into the crook of his arm and began walking.

Patrick seemed harmless, and Sophie took no offence. She felt a bit shy to be escorted by such a good-looking man, but she was comfortable.

"I have never been in a tearoom," she whispered.

"I have never been to this grand one either," he said as he smiled down at her. "It's our little secret, then?"

Sophie was taken aback. Patrick had also never been there, but he was approaching it with all the confidence in the world.

"You've definitely never been here?"

"Never."

"Aren't you afraid to go into such a posh tearoom?"

"Not at all. I can afford to pay my bill, and I have a beautiful lady on my arm."

He gently cupped her hand with his spare one and squeezed it.

"Are you always this fearless? Mr Gallagher?"

"Always."

The door to the tea emporium was opened by the maître d', who confirmed their booking and called a waiter to escort them to their table.

The grand tearoom was ornate and intimate. Being wintery, the light was already starting to fade on the day. The lamps had been lit, and a warm glow settled over the rich rosewood furniture. The curtains were white lace that reflected the lamp light perfectly and brightened the room when it was dark. In the summer, Sophie guessed they would provide a lovely dappled shade on a hot day. Although it was cold outside, the sun gave an impression of what it might be like in summer. The walls were painted light blue. Floor-to-ceiling panels lined the wall, each with a hand-painted mural of the most spectacular woodland scenes. Patrick noticed his guest's eyes darting from one ornate feature to another.

"Gosh. It's magnificent," she whispered.

"Very."

"It doesn't feel like winter inside here at all. It's so bright. And the murals make you feel like you're outside, enjoying the fine weather!" said Sophie in awe.

"Thank goodness for that. A little less winter would be welcome, don't you think?" he joked.

"I can't believe I work in a laundry, and you are happy to be seen here with me."

"Is there something wrong with you? Are you a criminal?"

Patrick looked stern.

"Do you have an embarrassing ailment?"

"Not at all," replied Sophie, taken aback by his demeanour.

"Jolly good, then you fit in perfectly."

The table was set with a white tablecloth, ornate silverware, and sparkling crystal. The blue-and-white porcelain blended perfectly with the hue of the walls. The delicate cups and saucers were the most beautiful she had ever seen.

Patrick picked up a teacup and looked underneath it.

"Spode," he said casually. "If you are posh, you know these things without looking—although I still can't tell them from a Wedgwood most of the time."

"It's beautiful," sighed Sophie.

"One day, when you marry, you can buy a service just like this for your home."

Sophie blushed, then laughed.

"I doubt it. I will never have this finery. I'll still be using a dented white enamel mug with its chipped dark blue rim."

"You need to dream a little more, Sophie Bryant. Dreams do come true."

"You are good at telling these jokes. Are you on the stage?" she chirped to deflect the comment.

"Not at all. If my ma had not been a dreamer, I would still be in the slums."

Patrick had a fleeting moment of guilt.

"She sounds fascinating. Do you see her often?"

"Ah. That was a long time ago," he muttered. "A different life."

There was a pause. Sophie guessed that his mother was not a topic he felt comfortable discussing.

"I wanted to invite you for tea after we met in the laundry."

His smile was dazzling.

"Stop it," she whispered, "you're just being silly now."

"Not at all. I can remember the moment clearly. Your creamy skin was slightly flushed from the heat. Your striking eyes sparkled. That delicate curl to your hair. I have been smitten with you since I gave you the letter."

"Smitten?"

"Terribly smitten," he confessed with a grin.

Sophie's face reflected his cheeriness back at him. *'Smitten, eh, Patrick Gallagher? You dark horse!'* She felt her face reddening again.

"What will happen now that Miss Holmes is dismissed?" asked Sophie, embarrassed and trying to change the subject.

"Miss Bryant! I refuse to discuss work when I am not at the place. So today, we will just have a jolly old time and enjoy each other's company? Agreed?"

"Are you ever serious?" Sophie challenged.

"Sometimes," he laughed, "otherwise never."

She had never been in the company of such a cheerful individual, apart from perhaps Lady Leticia. Usually, people spent hours complaining about their lot, but not this man.

"How is it that you are always so happy?"

The smile slipped from the Irishman's face briefly.

"My mother gave up a lot for me to be happy. I wouldn't be honouring her if I was miserable."

Sophie's suspicious about his mother were true. He'd lost her.

"She died peacefully in her bed—I was with her til the very end."

"I am so sorry—."

"No matter. Life goes on, as they say. But I owe her a debt of gratitude, and I intend to repay it one day when I have my own family. She would have made such a fuss of her grandchildren. More of a fuss than she made of me, no doubt!"

His face brightened as he nibbled nervously at his lower lip.

"You want a family?"

"Oh yes, I want children. I mean, they sometimes drive you mad, but I still think it's worth it."

"I'm an only child," Sophie told him. "I wish I had a brother or a sister."

"Do you plan on seeing your parents at Christmas?"

"Not if I can help it. Why do you think I put a few hundred miles between us!"

As they learned more about each other, Patrick and Sophie didn't stop talking and laughing. If the conversation took a more sombre tone, the other one introduced some levity. Sitting opposite her, Patrick knew he was correct. Notwithstanding the old brown dress, Sophie was the most beautiful woman in the room.

*

"Crikey, look at the time," said Sophie looking at the ivory dial of a nearby carriage clock. "I am not ready to return to the club and that dingy room."

Sophie looked disappointed.

"I can't say I'm itching to return either," he confessed.

"There is a music hall close by. It is called The Songbird. It's owned by a wonderful gentleman named Max, who puts on a pretty good show."

"Do people drink at music halls?" asked Sophie. "I am not one for the liquor. It reminds me of pa when he was in one of his dark slumps."

"Of course, they do," he laughed, "but you, young lady, don't have to do anything you don't want to. I will even order you a glass of milk if you so wish."

Looking for a cab, Patrick waved his arm in the air. As he stood on the kerb whistling, he seemed so full of life. She was delighted she would get to spend a little more time with him.

*

The music hall could have doubled as a circus. The energy and the spectacle were tremendous. Max waved at Patrick.

"He knows everyone," Patrick laughed.

Big-hearted Max sauntered over to Patrick and Sophie. He introduced himself to the girl and shook her hand.

"Do you know how long I have known this boy?"

Max pointed at Patrick. The old man had a strange accent, which Sophie couldn't place at all.

"I have known him for many years, and it's the first time he has come here with a lady."

Max was smiling from ear to ear.

"Give over, Max," Patrick laughed. "You are telling the lovely Miss Bryant all my secrets."

"You know that I love romance. Love is a wonderful thing. Love first, then family, then health, work, and wealth."

Sophie had never heard a man speak of these things before.

"Don't let this lady get away. I can see that you belong together."

"I have been thinking that all night, but I can't tell her that."

"How so?" enquired Max, frowning.

"I am here, you know!" Sophie interrupted. "And we have only just met."

"That means nothing!"

Max threw his arms in the air and then patted Patrick on the back.

"Congratulations, my boy, congratulations on your engagement."

Sophie was taken aback. Her eyes were huge, and she couldn't believe they were having this conversation right before her.

"Thank you, Max. Now, I only need to have her say, 'I do'."

"Oh, she will, she will," Max said, laughing deeply.

Sophie wondered what on earth she had got herself into but was grateful that it was tremendous fun.

A young woman came onto the stage. She was an exotic beauty with dark skin and black hair. She sang like a nightingale, and the audience was rapt by her beauty and voice.

"She is lovely," sighed Max.

Patrick and Sophie nodded simultaneously.

Max lifted his arm again and pointed his cigar at a lonely figure standing in the wings. The man was the same age as Patrick. He watched the girl perform and didn't take his eyes off her for a second.

"You know my son, David?" asked Max

"Of course I do," answered Patrick.

"Do you see how he watches the girl?"

Patrick nodded and smiled.

"He's got the same problem as you. He's in love with her but hasn't realised it yet," laughed Max. "I wish they would marry. I need grandchildren to keep me young."

*

When the plush curtains swished together, and the spectacular performance came to an end, Sophie knew that soon she would be back in the squalid little room she shared with Poppy. She decided she would not breathe a word of what happened today to her roommate, no matter how much Poppy might plead to know every little detail. She hoped it wouldn't be too long until she enjoyed another day like this one. It would give her the strength to carry on at the club.

*

"This has been the best day of my life," Sophie whispered. "Thank you."

"Get away with you. It's not." Patrick corrected. "—Your best day will be your wedding day."

"Stop being silly."

"And no registry office for you, my dear. You will marry in a church, in a beautiful dress. Your hair won't be twisted under a hat, but it'll be loose and wild, with pretty fresh flowers pinned into it."

Sophie wanted to believe everything he told her, but she was reticent. Patrick Gallagher made her feel like she was the only woman in the universe. Sophie was a level-headed girl, and as much as she wished for romance, she was afraid to dream of it. Like she had said to Poppy once before, *'men like this don't marry girls like us.'*

*

Patrick glanced at his fob watch. Ten o'clock. There wasn't long to get Sophie back before her curfew of eleven.

"We need to get back to the castle, Cinderella," he teased.

Gallagher steered Sophie out of the theatre with his hand gently touching her on the small of her back. They both felt a delicious tingle. The air was damp with a light drizzle. The streets shone under the gas lamps.

"Wait here," Patrick said before standing in the street and hailing a cab.

Guilt gripped her throat as Sophie started to cover the cost of the day.

"You can't walk in the rain," he said as he pushed her into the cab before she could protest.

The coach rattled along the cobbles. This was another experience she seldom had. She had always thought cab rides were too expensive and preferred to save pennies by walking. She was so at ease with Patrick that when he took her hand, she didn't flinch.

"Would you like to accompany me to the opera one evening?" Patrick asked her.

"Yes! And no!"

"Well, which yes or no do you mean?"

"I work in a laundry. I get one weekend off a month if I don't damage anything."

"I shall wait for you," he teased.

"Oh, do stop now," she laughed. "Men like you don't take laundry maids to the opera."

"Oh, but they do, Sophie. I promise you that they do."

*

Patrick helped Sophie out of the cab and escorted her down the alley that led to the servant's entrance. When they reached the gate, he looked up at the sign's skull and crossbones and felt his heart lurch. She turned her face up to look at him. She wanted to thank him for the beautiful day. Patrick didn't allow her to say a word. He looked into her eyes and then slowly bent over and kissed her.

"What if someone finds out?" Sophie whispered in horror.

"I don't believe in secrets, Sophie Bryant. I am falling in love with you, and you can tell everybody."

13

MR AND MRS AUSTEN

Lady Maria Holshausen Gresham was a picture of composure as she sat across from her husband at the breakfast table, studying him carefully. Anthony Gresham hardly ever came home these days, except if there was a social function that would benefit his political career. Anthony had long since stopped making excuses for his absence, and Maria didn't miss him enough to raise the subject.

Maria was aloof, but she was not stupid. She noted that her husband had a new swagger in his step. Since he had lived in London at the St Regis Club and participated in politics, he had gained confidence. If Maria had been a commoner, she would have used the term *'cocky'*.

Anthony no longer shrunk away from Maria. He was confrontational. She was irritated by her husband's bombastic tendencies but attributed his change in behaviour to his newfound career.

He wiped his mouth with a napkin and set it aside. He put his elbows on the table, leaned forward, and addressed his wife.

"The Prime Minister called me aside yesterday," Anthony paused.

Maria didn't say a word.

"It has become evident that I will be appointed to the Foreign Office after the elections."

Maria nodded her perfect head.

"Oh, for goodness' sake, say something, woman!"

"Congratulations Anthony. You have always steered away from the political arena. I am delighted you are approaching your newfound career so ambitiously," she answered sarcastically.

Anthony wanted to throw his teacup at her.

"I will be home more frequently. Of course, I will still spend some time at the club, but for the most part, I will be here. Please instruct the housekeeper to have my study cleaned and dusted as soon as possible."

"Certainly," Maria replied.

As he gave the command, Anthony was reminded of his room at the club and Poppy's late-night visits. He didn't love the naïve servant but had become accustomed to the girl's comfort and release. He had considered hiring Poppy as a servant in his home, but Maria would be suspicious if he insisted upon it. She would realise that he was using the girl. He wasn't bothered about further deterioration in his marriage, but an affair could cost him his career. This new vulnerability was an imposition. If he wished to keep a woman, he would need to be discreet.

"We will have to appear a happily married couple," continued Anthony.

"Yes," replied Maria.

"Say something more than yes!" he yelled, thumping the table and making the crockery rattle.

"I am sorry that I can't be enthusiastic about our future, Anthony. Although, as you know, in our class, we don't need to love a man to become his wife."

"What do you mean by that?"

"I may have taken your name, but I don't share your values. I may be your wife and play a part in public, but I don't need to do it in private."

Anthony was astounded. His newly found confidence at the hands of Poppy emboldened him. Throughout his marriage, he had deferred to his wife's rules.

"There is one thing that you do have to do. I want a son," Anthony said in a steely tone.

"No."

"I want a son, and I don't care how many confinements it takes."

Maria got up and turned her back on him. She left the breakfast room, softly closing the door behind her.

Anthony was furious. He stood up from the table, marched across the room and yanked the door open. The sound echoed through the house. He pounded up the staircase like a bull and followed his wife into their bedroom. Maria heard him behind her and turned around.

"You will have my child."

Her cool gaze infuriated him further. Anthony's wrath overcame him. It was fury, not lust, that drove him. He pushed Maria onto the bed roughly.

"Let me show you how a child is really made.."

Anthony lifted her dress. He pinned her down with all his weight. Maria lay as still as a corpse, knowing it was more demeaning for him than if she had fought back.

*

Afterwards, Anthony couldn't believe that he had done it. After tolerating so much frustration, the man had taken his wife by force. Still, the chance of having a son and heir was worth it.

As he rolled off Maria, his mind skipped back to Poppy. He had to find a way to rid himself of the relationship that could destroy him. It would be best that she simply disappeared. He suspected Poppy knew that there was no future for them. Although she was besotted with him, if he explained it correctly, she would understand. And she was so poor, it wouldn't take much to buy her silence. He could easily pay her enough money and send her off to begin a new life in a colony or a town very far away from London. Problem solved.

Lord Anthony Gresham began to solidify his plan. He decided he couldn't risk giving her the bad news at the St Regis Club. What if she became hysterical? The lower classes were capable of anything when pushed to the limit and didn't keep a stiff upper lip. It dawned on him why women were outlawed by the clubs. This was precisely the type of situation one could ill afford socially. Simply put, he should have patronised a discreet high-class brothel if he wanted the kind of experience he had with Poppy and then returned to the lounge to be with his clique of friends.

*

It was Sunday, and Lord Anthony Gresham was lying with Poppy in his arms. The girl had served her once more purpose, but it was becoming dull and repetitive as with all the other women he had known. He wouldn't find it too challenging to court somebody of the upper class who was experienced in the more erotic arts of lovemaking. Once he had impregnated Maria, he was definitely going to find one.

*

The Doggett Arms Inn lay in the heart of the docklands. This area pulsed with activity and was so densely populated that one face melded into the next striking everyone invisible. The working-class uniform consisted of a ruddy brown or grey jacket, the same colour trousers and an unpressed shirt. Most men wore a flat cap. They were easy enough to work in.

Gresham was attired in this commoner's uniform as he guided Poppy Patterson down the pier to the little inn situated in a narrow side street barely wider than a wheelbarrow. It was the first time Poppy had slept at an inn, and the idea sounded exciting when Anthony mentioned it.

The inn keeper introduced himself as Jesse. He showed them up a rickety flight of stairs and onto a narrow landing where every second floorboard was missing.

"What's your name, gov?" asked Jesse.

"Mr and Mrs Austen," Gresham replied.

'I bet you are. You speak far too posh for a normal bloke about these parts.'

"It's shoddy," commented Poppy. "Even me ma's old cottage is better than this."

Jesse gave Poppy a look, his suspicions confirmed. *'Why you cheeky little wench! And that accent is common and from somewhere up north.'* He had seen many a gentleman with a loose woman in tow under the pretence of being married.

"Now, now, it's a place for us to get some rest. We have a long journey ahead of us." Lord Gresham said, trying to appease her. "It's only for one night."

Jesse showed them into the small, musty room. The rain had leaked through the ceiling, and the cornices were green. Anthony Gresham prayed they wouldn't spend too much time there, as the mould was sufficient to cause his death.

Jesse closed the door, and Anthony set about undressing Poppy. For some reason, something seemed different about her, but he pushed the thought out of his mind. He was looking forward to her being emotionally vulnerable after he had made love to her, knowing, as always, it was the best time to manipulate her feelings. During the act of love, he repeatedly told her how he adored her and that she was beautiful. Only once he had satisfied himself and had young Poppy lying pliable in his arms did he dare take on the subject of separation.

"My darling," he whispered, stroking Poppy's hair tenderly. "I have news to tell you."

He pushed her hair off her face and looked into her eyes. He had thought carefully about how he would tell her, deciding it would be best if he appeared a victim of circumstance.

"The Prime Minister called me aside a few days ago."

"The Prime Minister?" Poppy gasped, and her eyes widened.

"Yes, I am surprised it was not Her Majesty the Queen. The situation is dire."

"Do you speak to the Queen?"

Poppy was astounded.

"Yes, my darling, regularly," he lied.

"What is it? What has happened? Are you in trouble then?"

"Not at all, my dear. It is far worse than that," Anthony exaggerated.

"Tell me what has happened."

"It is terrible, terrible. I can't go through with it. But the country desperately needs me."

"Is there going to be a war?" Poppy asked.

"There very well could be if I don't help the Prime Minister. The whole of England may be threatened."

"Where are you going?"

"Poppy, you know that I am being appointed to the Foreign Office?"

Poppy nodded.

"The Prime Minister has insisted I spend more time at my home in Mayfair. I need to present a respectable front. We need Maria's influence to prevent war between Britain and Hungary."

"What!" exclaimed Poppy. "The Prime Minister is forcing you to return to that horrible woman. The one that you hate? The one who is so beastly to you?"

Lord Anthony Gresham put on a great act of being forlorn. He even managed to get his eyes to water.

"What will happen to us? I love you!"

Anthony clasped her to his chest.

"I will find a way for us. I promise I will. But you have to promise me that you won't tell a soul. It would endanger our whole nation—and it will endanger you."

"I promise, Anthony, I promise."

"Don't tell any of your friends. And never tell Sophie, do you hear me? I know you two are very close."

"Of course, I won't. Besides, we're not such good friends anymore. We had a bit of a falling out."

Anthony was relieved. He was just about to push her away from him and leave for good when she spoke.

"I also have some news, good news, for you. Maybe this will give you strength while we are apart?"

"What is it, my sweet?"

" I know how much you have always wanted a child," Poppy began.

Instinctively Anthony knew what would come next.

"I'm going to have a baby!" Poppy chirruped, "I am going to have the son that you have longed for!"

"God Almighty!"

Gresham felt as if someone had punched the wind out of him. He sat on the edge of the bed, completely naked. It was frosty cold, but he didn't feel anything. Poppy had delivered a blow that he was ill-prepared for.

"Are you happy that you are going to be a father?"

Anthony was speechless. He didn't know what to say or do. He stood up. She slid up beside him, rubbing her belly against him.

"I can go and live somewhere, say I am widowed. You can visit us. I'll need a bit of money to get set up, of course, but I promise I will pay you back."

Anthony couldn't keep his composure, and he became furious. Jesse could hear Anthony shouting but couldn't make out the words. Finally, Anthony grabbed Poppy by her throat and leaned in. She scrabbled at his chest, her eyes bulging.

"I don't want a stupid mongrel. What makes you think I want a child with a low-class commoner from some god-forsaken place I have never heard of. I will pay you to get rid of it. You can go to a woman I have heard of who does these things. You must get rid of it. Or I will."

Poppy pushed him away from her, and his hands fell to his sides.

"It's too far gone," she cried, "I will die if they do it now."

"Fiddlesticks! It's only been a few months."

"I thought you would be pleased."

"Pleased? I could kill you right now!"

His hands sprang up and began to throttle her.

"Stop. It." Poppy sobbed. "I love you."

He took her by the shoulders and shook her roughly.

"Who have you told."

"Nobody, I promise you."

"Not even your friend, Sophie Bryant?" he demanded, shaking her again.

"No. No. I would never tell anyone. I promise you."

Anthony shoved Poppy backwards. She fell, stumbling over a small wooden chair, knocking her head on the floor with a loud crack. Poppy sat up dazed and saw the rogue getting dressed. It was then he realised his mistake. If he was going to control Poppy effectively, he would have to turn the charm back on.

"Oh, I am sorry, my darling. It's the shock. And the stress of Westminster. You know how much I have yearned for a child. The best thing is to keep quiet. Let me sort this out. I will do what I can from afar. Once this wretched political situation is solved, we will be together. I promise. If someone suspects you're pregnant, I suggest you make them think the father is another member of staff but don't name names."

"Of course. Anything for you, Anthony."

The cad helped her up, kissed her tenderly, then cupped her belly and kissed that too. If Poppy knew the truth, she would have been sickened. Lord Gresham had no conscience. The only person he could ever think of was himself.

When he got downstairs, Jesse stared at him. Anthony put his hand in his pocket and pulled out a pound note. He threw it across the counter at Jesse.

"Keep your mouth shut. If you know what's good for you."

Anthony escaped onto the street and into the crowd. Upstairs, Poppy was distraught, inconsolable, as she dragged her clothes back on, snivelling and weeping. She went down and passed Jesse at the counter. Her face was tear-stained, and he could see that she was troubled.

"You tarts never learn now, do you?" he called after her as she walked past.

Sophie turned around and returned to where he stood, her head a mess of tangled thoughts.

"Show some respect. That is Lord Anthony Gresham. I'm not a tart! I am Miss Poppy Patterson. His lordship loves me, and I will have his child," she continued. "He is a powerful man, and he will have you murdered if I ask him to. Mind your manners."

Jesse Cooper couldn't believe his luck. He had as good as scored the jackpot at the races. His future was secure. It was simple. He would either blackmail Lord Gresham or talk to the press.

*

It was dark, and Poppy trudged from St Giles to St James Square. The day that she had so looked forward to had ended in misery. Poppy couldn't understand what angered Anthony Gresham. He had told her he loved her, and she was sure the child would make him happy once it arrived. He just needed to give it a chance to sink in. She knew it might shock him, but she hadn't anticipated such an adverse reaction. She buttoned her coat and pulled her shawl close around her. Poppy hoped that Lord Anthony Gresham's temper would have abated by the time she went to him at midnight.

Poppy climbed the steps to her quarters. It was well after eleven, and she was surprised that no one had accosted her for being late. As her pregnancy progressed, she noticed how much more exhausted she was from a long walk. She hoped her sweetheart would pay for a room or flat where she and the baby could stay. She also prayed that nobody would spot the bump that would soon start to show if she wasn't careful.

*

Poppy opened the door to her quarters and saw Sophie stretched out on her bed. Sophie was smiling from ear to ear.

"Poppy, I need to tell you about my day out," began Sophie.

"Oh, what did you do?"

"Poppy, can you believe that Mr Gallagher took me out for tea."

"What?"

"He said it was to make up for the horrid manner Miss Holmes treated me."

"And you went with him, all alone with no chaperone?"

"We never need to go anywhere with a chaperone these days. Since when is a maid appointed a chaperone?"

"What made someone like you think you had a shot with Patrick Gallagher?"

Poppy pouted. She envied her friend's happiness and wanted to crush her spirit. Sophie was disappointed with her friend's response.

"I thought you would be happy for me?"

"So, you think that Mr Gallagher is a proper Irish gent, do you? Let me give you some advice, Sophie, stay away from him. You're not the only woman here who he has charmed."

"Who are you to tell me to stay away from Patrick?" demanded Sophie.

"So, it's Patrick, not *'Mr Gallagher'* anymore? Miss Holmes was right that he is a ladies' man."

There were no grounds for Poppy's accusations whatsoever, but being cruel and poisonous helped her forget Gresham's awful behaviour.

"I might not know where to, but I do know you disappear every night, Poppy. Maybe the gossips will share what you're up to? So, perhaps you should be worried more about your conduct than me?"

"So, you want to know where I go to? Here's a clue!" Poppy blurted out. "Perhaps I know Patrick better than you think?"

Sophie sat straight up in her bed.

"What did you just say?"

"You think that you are so high and mighty, Sophie. You know nothing. You're the same naïve girl I met at Langford Manor. This is the big city, not a place for stupid girls like you who will believe anything a man tells her."

"Patrick's intentions towards me are honest and genuine. How dare you suggest it's him you run off to!"

Poppy replied with a breathy voice that did little to soften the barbed comment.

"Believe what you like. I know where I go. Not you. And what's more, it's amazing! He's amazing. And I can't wait to see him again."

Poppy lay down on her bed. She put her hands on her belly for comfort. At that moment, she hated smug old

Sophie so much she could have shoved a knife into her heart.

Sophie was shattered. She turned around and faced the wall, so Poppy couldn't see the tears blinding her vision. She had a flicker of a thought. It was too horrible to consider, but still, it filled her mind. If Poppy was telling the truth, then Patrick Gallagher had taken her for a fool.

*

It was well past midnight when Poppy got up. Sophie heard her open the door and leave. She had the desire to follow her, but what good would that do? Would she go to Patrick's quarters and fight over him with her best friend? Never! She lay heartsore and humiliated. She counted the few coppers she had hidden under her mattress and decided to hand in her notice the following morning and return to Langford Manor on the cheapest third-class train when she received her next monthly pay packet. She should've left the horrible club months ago. Nothing but drudgery and heartache had come of their appointments. She had lost the benefit of the nurturing support and watchful eye of Lady Letitia, she had been silly enough to be hoodwinked by a cad, and she had fallen out with her best friend. The whole thing was an awful mistake.

Poppy followed the usual route to her lover's room. She tried the door, but it was locked. She watched the door from the servant's corridor for two hours. It was almost five o'clock in the morning when she went slumped off to her room, believing that Lord Gresham was probably lying in the arms of his beautiful wife.

*

Poppy was at her post by eight o'clock. She looked terrible. She had black rings under her eyes, red-rimmed from the stress of the day before. Mrs Tremarie was sure that the silly girl had been drinking heavily the night before.

> "By the way, Patterson, you have no need to clean room 17 today. Lord Gresham will no longer be staying here as much as he used to. He has been appointed to the Foreign Office and will spend more time at his home entertaining dignitaries in Mayfair."

For a moment, Poppy's whole world changed. Finally, she suspected the devastating truth of the matter. Lord Gresham might have used her and never wanted to see her again. Then she told herself everything was fine, and she had to keep up appearances for the good of the country, just like he'd told her to.

14

RUMOUR

Sophie was determined to never confide or speak to Poppy again. Poppy was no longer the energetic free spirit that she had met at Langford Manor. Her former friend looked anxious and sullen. Also, she was prone to sudden outbursts in which she would insult Sophie as agonisingly as she could.

Now that Sophie suspected Poppy's relationship with Patrick Gallagher, she couldn't look at Poppy without feeling betrayed. The poor girl was a tangle of emotions. What if Patrick had turned on the charm and wooed her friend, just as he had with her? Being more bohemian in her outlook, it was understandable if Poppy succumbed and chose to take things further. After all, there was very little else to make life at the club bearable.

Round and round, her mind went. Patrick seemed so honourable. It didn't make sense. If he was such a lothario, why take her to the tearooms and not somewhere more private where he could have his way with her? She began to suspect Poppy's suggestion was merely a ruse to throw her off the scent of the real culprit. Then, she recalled that when she had gossiped about Lord Anthony Gresham once, Poppy had responded viciously, presumably to hide the truth.

He had berated one of the waiters at dinner once for some minor mistake and had him sacked. Sophie had said how callous Anthony had been, yet Poppy defended him. He, too, had dark hair.

Sophie remembered the incident clearly. How could she have been so stupid? She had suspected the wrong man all along. She finished dressing and went to her station in the laundry. She was miserable with the outcome of the events but also excited that she was going back to Langford Manor. While it had been nice to be courted by Patrick, they had no future. These days, a slice of quiet country life was what Sophie wanted more than anything.

She had penned a long letter to Letitia Langford the night before. She only had to suffer the club for another few weeks.

*

Patrick Gallagher sat behind his desk with a dreamy look in his eyes. He enjoyed his time with Sophie and was trying to recall every moment. He was wondering if she would see him again. He decided that Sophie Bryant was bright. She had a good sense of humour, and he was sure she had not taken offence at his suggestion to take her out to the theatre. He had not been teasing when he told her that he liked her. Neither was he lying when he told her he would take her to the opera, nor when he confessed he was smitten from the moment he delivered the letter to her in the laundry. His thoughts were interrupted by Mr Aldridge standing in the doorway.

"Good morning, sir," he greeted as he smiled at the old man. "This is a treat. Come on in, take a seat."

Aldridge always admired Patrick's impeccable manners.

"I have a letter for you. It was delivered to my desk by Lord Gresham's secretary. It must be important if it couldn't be delivered by an office boy."

"So early on a Monday morning," grumbled Patrick. "I have hardly woken up yet."

Gallagher unfolded the quickly scribbled note.

Meet me at the lounge in Claridge's

15h 00

Anthony

'Typical aristocracy. Inconsiderate and demanding.' His fondness for Anthony Gresham had waned of late, and suffering through an afternoon with him would be torture. Yet, Patrick was still intrigued that he had been summoned. Considering that Anthony wouldn't be spending as much time in his room at the club, it was perhaps to be expected. He worked primarily from his

study in Mayfair then or at the Palace of Westminster. Perhaps Anthony wanted to be updated on facts and figures or on the recent gossip in the club? He was still an owner of the place, after all.

Patrick would never have selected Claridge's as a meeting place. Instead, he would have preferred to have a few pints at the pub around the corner at the Red Lion on Whitehall.

*

Gallagher strode through the front doors into the marble lobby. He cut a fine figure in his black suit. Several heads turned, not because he wore fine clothing, but because he was a commanding figure, tall and handsome. Although he made sure he used the suit extensively, he hadn't yet made peace with paying a king's ransom for a set of clothes tailored on Savile Row.

He found Lord Anthony sitting in the lounge bar's dark, quiet corner. Usually, Gresham would have been the centre of attention at the bar counter, and there would be a flourish of activity around him. But not today.

The two men shook hands. Patrick sat down at the small round table, which probably would have cost him a year's salary to purchase. Gresham acknowledged Patrick and lifted his glass in salute.

"Irishman."

"Anthony," Patrick greeted with a nod.

Gallagher noted that Anthony Gresham's mood boasted formality and that the man looked sombre. His iciness towards his former friend melted a little. Perhaps Gresham's recent unkindness was routed in strife rather than meanness?

"I am flattered by your invitation. A few drinks will be nice. It's been a while."

"Yes, well, it's a little more serious than a few drinks between friends, I'm afraid." Lord Gresham confessed.

"Have you tired of politics so quickly, Tony? I thought it was going well?"

The remark seemed to annoy Gresham, who was not in the mood for banter.

"Not at all. I am finding my position challenging."

The waiter took their order, and Anthony spoke when the man was out of earshot.

"It's a bit delicate. Remind me, I don't need to lecture you on confidentiality, do I?"

"I don't think so," snapped Patrick, irritated by the aristocrat's arrogance.

"What is your greatest dream, Irishman? A large home and an obedient, dedicated wife. Perhaps a company that specialises in a few special accounts for people who can afford to pay you well."

It was a rhetorical question. Patrick was maddened by the suggestion of an obedient wife. He didn't want a woman who would kowtow to him. He wanted a soulmate. Gallagher didn't answer and let the man continue.

"Your future can be secure."

Patrick bowed his head to one side and frowned.

"Cut to the chase, man. Do you want me to do some extra work for you?"

"In a manner of speaking, yes."

Anthony took a sip of his drink and continued.

"You must understand that this can never get out. You must never mention our arrangement to anyone at the club. Any sort of scandal will destroy me. I trust that this will be a gentlemen's agreement between us. There can be no written contract. It is too sensitive."

"I don't recall us agreeing to anything yet.".

Sir Anthony Gresham's constant stream of selfish assumptions grated on Anthony's nerves. As Patrick waited for the man to continue, the silence between them was awkward. Anthony squinted around the room and looked over his shoulder.

"I am in a bit of trouble, Irishman," Anthony whispered.

He leaned forward and met Patrick's eyes.

"The chambermaid, the little thing I've been, uhm.... You know the girl. Poppy. I've mentioned her before." he laughed grimly. "Well, I've had her in my bed for months. Seems to have got the impression I had a real thing for her, which is, of course, ridiculous."

Patrick nodded slowly, appalled by Anthony's boasting and lack of shame.

"She's got herself good and pregnant. With someone of the lower-class, of course, it could be anyone's child, but she knows enough about me to prove she has been in my bed and, at the very least, implicate me in some sordid adventures."

He winked slyly.

Patrick was confused. Why was Anthony Gresham telling him this? It had the power to ruin him if it got out. Gresham was surely powerful enough to pull a few strings with someone outside his usual circle?

"I can't believe it. The little thing gets pregnant in no time. Several months gone now, she is. My blasted wife and I have been married for much longer and nothing. Not the faintest whiff of a child. Now, this silly tart is up the duff.."

Patrick took a large gulp of his Scotch.

"If this gets out, I will lose my position in government," lamented Anthony. "Not to mention Maria. She and her father will destroy me. Imagine a commoner's illegitimate lovechild inheriting my title and my fortune. I will be the laughing stock of the country. I told the girl to get rid of it. I will pay, of course. She says it's far too late to do anything about it. Wants to keep it and for me to leave everything in Mayfair and live with her, which, as you know, is utterly preposterous."

Anthony was so anxious that he gulped down the rest of his Scotch in one mouthful and gestured he wanted to order another large one.

"What has this got to do with me, Anthony?"

"You're the only one who can get me out of this damned mess," Gresham cursed.

"How?"

"Marry her."

Patrick studied him aghast. The man was serious.

"What!"

"You will never need for anything. You will be set up for the rest of your life. You only have to keep the secret and marry the girl."

"I am not marrying her. Have you lost your mind?"

"You have done well, Irishman, but you are not a man of great means. This can be your saving grace," badgered Anthony trying desperately to convince Patrick.

"I don't need to be saved, Lord Gresham," Patrick said formally.

"Name your price," Lord Anthony persisted.

"You want to pay me to marry a woman whom I don't love? Then, raise your child as my own? No!"

"You want to marry for love? Have you gone mad, man? I thought I could count upon your loyalty," Anthony muttered with bitterness in his voice.

Patrick had said everything he wanted to. There was no need to say anything more.

"You're happy for this child to grow up without a father, Irishman, when you know what that feels like?"

"I have no qualms with the child, sir, and I feel very sorry for the young woman. But you have ruined both their futures by denying accepting responsibility. If you want to make amends, pay for Poppy to leave and start again. I am sure you can buy her silence if you are sufficiently menacing."

Anthony's eyes were now dark slits, indicating he was furious.

"I told the young woman to name you as the father if she is pressed to reveal the child's paternity," Anthony lied. "I told her you will look after her from now on. Of course, I will pay you, but she won't know that. I want nobody to trace the money back to me. Let's just say I add a little extra to my monthly club funds, and you can pocket the balance."

"You what? Do you want me to make fraudulent transactions against the St Regis club? Well, I won't. No amount of money would ever be worth it. And I won't enter into any relationship with your mistress."

Patrick wanted to climb over the table and belt the smarmy grin off Anthony's face but managed to stave it off.

"She is not my mistress. She is a little whore."

All that came to Patrick's mind was that Anthony's selfish, immoral ways would ruin his future with Sophie. Gallagher's fists were balled, and he was ready for the fight.

"Think carefully, Irishman. This can cost you your reputation and your job. As your employer, I can make life very difficult for you. It can be tough being dismissed and lacking references."

"You swine, Gresham!"

Anthony was furious. He slammed his glass down on the table. Everyone standing at the bar turned around to stare at the kerfuffle. He put on a false smile and retook his seat.

"Patrick, will you at least consider the offer?"

The Irishman couldn't believe the man's persistence.

"I never want to discuss this again, Lord Gresham. Never!"

Patrick Gallagher set his unfinished drink down on the expensive table. He pushed his chair back, stood up, then fumbled in his pocket and pulled out some money. He set it down next to his glass.

"Take your money back, Irishman," Anthony Gresham told him. "The drinks were on me."

"Thank you, sir. But I can afford my own drinks."

Anthony was sour. Patrick Gallagher then turned his back on Lord Gresham and walked away. He left the politician as he had found him, alone and desperate, and still with his delicate and pressing problem to solve.

*

Poppy's pregnancy had become an open secret. Depressingly, it seemed like her stomach had grown overnight, and her baggy clothes could no longer hide her swollen belly. Every time she was alone, she feared suffering abuse.

"Who is your husband, Poppy?" the other girls would goad her.

"When is the bairn coming?"

"You're just a hussy, so you are."

"I wouldn't trust you anywhere close to my fella."

"Come now, lass, who is the father?"

Poppy continued to deny the pregnancy for as long as she could, but eventually, it was apparent. The casual, cruel comments the other girls meted out became relentless persecution.

All her colleagues tormented Poppy until she couldn't bear it any longer. She hated everybody around her. She would lie in bed every night plotting revenge and fantasizing as to how she would poison each one to bring about a slow and torturous death.

One afternoon, Mrs Tremarie called her to the office. The woman was ruthless

"Your last day will be this Saturday. After Mr Aldridge has paid you, you will leave, not to return."

Poppy knew that it was coming.

"You seem to understand the ways of the world," she observed, looking at Poppy's stomach. "I am sure you know exactly what to do to look after yourself. By the way, my dear, do you know who the father is?"

Poppy stared at the woman and nodded her head.

"We may consider helping you if you name him. I will ask Mr Aldridge to include a little extra in your severance pay," Mrs Tremarie coaxed her. "You do understand we need to know which staff member is responsible."

Poppy didn't dare tell Mrs Tremarie that she was carrying Lord Gresham's child. She had promised him that she would protect him. Poppy was hopelessly in love with Anthony, and she was still convinced that he had only been cruel because the country depended upon him. *'As soon as he has done his duty to the nation, he will do his duty to me, won't he? Everything will work out fine.'*

*

Lord Anthony sat behind his desk in his study at the grand Mayfair mansion that he had to share with his cold wife. He was furious. He had expected far better from his friend, the Irishman. Any sane man would have jumped at the opportunity of financial security, but not Patrick Gallagher. He could only hope that Poppy would stay firm in her promise to keep her mouth shut. He decided his best option was to send her a bit of money for a train ticket and hope she assumed he would meet her there. She was to name the Irishman the father if she was forced to confess the child's paternity. He was sure the funds would be an incentive to obey his instructions and a false indication of his undying dedication to her.

Anthony felt as if he no longer had a grasp on his life. His wife despised him. He had been forced into a career in the Foreign Office that he didn't want. His mistress was pregnant, and the man he had asked to marry her had refused point blank.

Lord Gresham's main objective was to prevent a scandal. If anyone found out about the child, he would be ruined. If the child was a son, it would cause the greatest upset. His vast fortune would legally pass to the illegitimate son of a commoner who had arrived from the netherworld to seek her fortune. It was not his fault that she had chosen to do it on her back. Anthony realised that he would have to deal with Poppy carefully if he wanted to buy her silence in the long term.

Anthony Gresham took a sheet of plain paper from his drawer and set it on his desk, grabbed his pen and began to write. He started with the date, then *'Dearest Poppy'*. He took his time wording it correctly, taking pains disguising his handwriting. He read his masterpiece once more, then stared into space, congratulating himself on his deviousness. It was perfect, except he made one fatal mistake. Still in his trance-like state, he signed his name at the bottom of the page with a proud flourish. He put his letter into a plain envelope and sealed it. Then, he whipped up the correspondence and threw it into the bottom drawer of his intricately carved desk. He would post it himself in the morning, thereby combatting the risk of being found out.

*

Mrs Tremarie made the most of Poppy's last few days at the club. Every day she chipped away at what was left of the girl's spirit, breaking her down one small step at a time, wishing she could make the stubborn girl divulge her secrets. Mrs Tremarie was prepared to torture a confession out of Poppy if she had to. She was confident that the child was sired by Lord Gresham. Knowledge was power, and Mrs Tremarie could negotiate herself a secure future with that morsel of information.

During the final days of her employment at the club, Poppy was slowly collapsing under the intense pressure and constant scrutiny of the staff. The mean-spirited servants made snide remarks under their breath. Others didn't even show that amount of respect. They just cursed Poppy to her face.

After a particularly tough morning shift, Mrs Tremarie called young Poppy into her office. She had tried all methods of prying and prodding to get the truth from Poppy, who still refused to say a word. But Mrs Tremarie also knew that most people could overcome any temptation except money.

"This is your last night with us," Mrs Tremarie lied kindly. "I wish things could have been different. You have been a hard worker."

Poppy nodded. She had expected the woman to be as stern as she usually was, so the change in tack was unsettling.

"We all feel so sad at your leaving, Poppy. You have been very valuable here."

Poppy was close to tears.

"This is likely your last night in safe quarters. It will be a lot more difficult from here on forward. The common lodging houses round this area are horrific."

Tears began to run down Poppy's face.

"We have taken up a little collection for you. It may help."

Poppy nodded.

"Thank you," she sniffed.

"Such a pity that you have been left like this, you are young, and men are lecherous."

Poppy had given the situation a lot of thought. She knew that what she was going to tell Mrs Tremarie would upset Sophie to her core. It would be a lie that would become the final nail in the coffin of their friendship. No matter how treacherous a decision it was, it still did the one thing that mattered to Poppy Patterson—it protected her dearest Anthony as he saved the nation.

Having no intention to be stuck in common lodgings or the workhouse, Poppy had toyed with the idea of picking a foreign name at random. That way, she could say that the father was away or at sea. There were plenty of men from overseas flowing through the Port of London. Then Poppy suspected it might be better to put a local man's name on the birth forms if she wanted any assistance from the local parish. One name stood out. Patrick Gallagher. He had a good income and could easily fund better lodgings for her. It was perfect. Little did she know that it would make no difference as to how the authorities or society would treat her. She was a fallen woman, and they would never allow her to forget it. Her child would be shunned forever for its mere fate of being conceived out of wedlock.

"You deserve to be cared for, my dear. I take it upon myself to ensure that the father of this child supports you. To whom must I call upon to get a stipend for you? My sister will take you in and care for you during your confinement," she said solemnly.

Mrs Tremarie passed Poppy a note with an address written on it. The naïve girl was shocked that the housekeeper would go to such lengths to help her.

"Thank you! Oh, thank you for being so kind," Poppy sobbed.

"No matter at all, my dear. Now, the name, please?"

"Patrick Gallagher, ma'am," Poppy stuttered.

Mrs Tremarie was taken aback. It was not the name that she was preparing herself to hear.

"What did you say? Who is the father?"

"Patrick Gallagher, ma'am."

In all her years, Mrs Tremarie had never been so surprised. She sat down abruptly and took a swig of her sweet tea. She had waited years to clip Patrick Gallagher's wings, and this was the perfect opportunity to do so. The woman shooed Poppy out of the door and closed it behind her. Mrs Tremarie allowed herself a quiet whoop and then sat down to plot her course.

15

DESPAIR

Mrs Tremarie wasted no time in subtly spreading the news that Patrick Gallagher had sired a child with the common chambermaid Poppy Patterson. She had a strategic plan and summoned someone with the reputation of being a gossip to her office. Late that evening, when things had wound down for the day, she invited the butler to have a glass of sherry with her. Making him swear that he wouldn't repeat a word, she told him that Patrick Gallagher was the father of Poppy's child.

When the butler met his lover later that evening, he repeated what Mrs Tremarie had told him. Word travelled from her to the young waiter, then to a barman in the club. The barman, in turn, told another maid. The gossip spread like wildfire. By noon it reached Mr Aldridge's ears. It was hardly two minutes past the hour when Mr Aldridge entered Patrick Gallagher's office.

"Patrick," he began without preamble.

"What has happened?"

"There is a rumour doing its rounds concerning you," Mr Aldridge said forthrightly.

"Oh! Is it my turn to be scandalised?"

"Yes," answered Mr Aldridge, "and it's a serious accusation."

"Be quick about it. What is it this time?"

Patrick was not in the mood for social politics. Mr Aldridge sat down in front of Patrick.

"You have been named as the father of Poppy Patterson's child."

Patrick closed his eyes and took in a deep breath.

"Which nosey parker has made this false accusation?"

"Miss Patterson herself, I'm afraid."

Patrick was too shocked to be furious. He was at an absolute loss for words. Nobody would ever believe the dynamics which had led to this moment. The story was too diabolical to be true.

"I have never been near that girl, Mr Aldridge."

Despite his earnest denial, the words sounded empty and unconvincing. Aldridge just nodded.

"This is going to cost me my job," muttered Patrick.

Patrick didn't say another word, and eventually, Mr Aldridge stood up to leave. When he reached the door, he turned around and looked at the young man.

"For what it's worth, I think you have been set up, Patrick. I will do whatever I can to help you."

"Thank you, old friend."

Mr Aldridge stepped out of the room and softly closed the door.

*

Sophie heard the news the moment she set foot in the laundry. The laundry maids were standing about in little pools of three and four, discussing the news that Poppy had alluded to Gallagher being the father of her child.

Sophie kept to one side and got on with her work. Although Poppy had hinted that she was having an affair with Patrick, Sophie never gave up hope that it was a lie. She knew that nobody knew of her and Patrick's short romance, yet she felt self-conscious and overcompensated by acting frantically busy. Some girls approached her for comment. After all, she shared a room with one half of the sordid couple.

The questions went on and on.

"Do you know when it happened?"

"Where did they meet?"

"How long have they been seeing each other?"

"Did Poppy go to Mr Gallagher's room every night?"

"Were the couple in love?"

"Were they going to marry?"

Sophie gave no comment, even though she wanted to shout the roof down about his innocence. Instead, she smiled politely and denied knowing anything, which was a convenient half-truth. All she had were strong suspicions about who Poppy's real dark-haired man was.

Sophie appeared nonchalant, but her stomach was as tight as a fist. Every movement she made and step she took felt animated and exaggerated. She forced herself to be casual because she didn't feel normal at all.

*

Sophie made her way to her room earlier than usual. It was ten-thirty. She knew she would have to face Poppy sooner or later but hoped to at least sleep on the matter first. She planned to sneak into bed and hide under the covers.

Sophie climbed the stairs. She was listless and emotionally drained from a long day of pretending to be unperturbed by the gossip. She opened the door and was shocked to see Poppy sitting on her bed facing her. Her case was packed, and she was fully clothed.

"It's late," was all Sophie could think of saying. "Where are you going to at this time of the night?"

"I have a place to stay until the baby comes. Patrick will give me a good amount of money," said Sophie, falsely referring to the funds Mrs Tremarie had collected for her.

Sophie felt tears welling in her eyes and had a pain in her chest.

"Where are you staying? Who was so kind?" She managed to ask.

"Mrs Tremarie."

Sophie guessed there was an ulterior motive for Mrs Tremarie's kindness. Poppy held the note in the air and wiggled it.

"This is the address," she said, self-assured.

Sophie took the note from her and read it. *'14 Rosemary Street St Giles'*, then handed it back to Poppy.

"You can't be surprised by the news," Poppy said confidently.

"I am."

"You can't say I lied to you," Poppy was playing her role perfectly.

"You told me that you fancied Lord Gresham."

"I said a dark-haired man. You just assumed Gresham. You know that a lord would never look at the likes of me. You told me that straight to my face. Do you remember?"

"So, you were slipping out to be with Patrick Gallagher every night?"

"Yes. He made me swear not to say a word to anyone. It just goes to show that I am good enough for a gentleman."

The lies came tumbling from Poppy like gushes of water from a pump. Sophie looked away, humiliated by what she was hearing. Poppy relished watching Sophie and knowing that she was hurting her.

"What about the child?" Sophie asked.

"We are going to get married."

It was an outright lie. Whether it was a part of Poppy's fantasy or belief in Lord Gresham's lies, what drove the ludicrous statement was unclear.

"Well then," said Sophie.

Poppy remained quiet.

"Well then, you had better be off. It's very late. I don't want you getting lost on the way to St Giles. It's not the safest of areas."

"I wanted to say goodbye to you. You know, no hard feelings and all."

Sophie opened the door for Poppy. Once, they had been the closest of friends. Now, she didn't know what to say and couldn't look at her face without feeling disgust. She had no desire to wish Poppy good luck. In her mind, *'good riddance'* was more appropriate.

Sophie sank down and sat on the edge of her bed. Her mind wandered into no-mans-land. She was unaware of time and space. She was deeply absorbed in memories of her and Patrick's brief and joyous time together. This was followed by questions and arguments. She pondered the events, hundreds of thoughts flashing through her mind at once, completely oblivious to her surroundings. She was jolted to reality by the sound of footsteps outside her door. Perhaps it was Patrick Gallagher sneaking to see her and assure her that everything was just a terrible lie. Alas, the sound of the footsteps receded. It wasn't Patrick, after all.

Sophie was cold. It was the early hours of the freezing London morning. She didn't have the desire to wash or put on her nightclothes. She climbed into bed fully clothed and slept fitfully, dreaming of Patrick, Poppy, and a dark, menacing house.

*

Poppy made her way through the bitterly cold London night, following the scant directions that Mrs Tremarie had given her. Eventually, she admitted that she was lost. She made her way toward Seven Dials, where some gipsies had set up camp in the marketplace. There were still fires going outside some of the caravans, and she summoned the courage to approach a man sitting next to one.

"Sir, please, can you help me?"

"What do you want from me?" the churlish man said.

"Nothing. I'm looking for Rosemary Street, that's all. Do you know it?"

"I've been spending the winter here for thirty years now. There is no Rosemary Street in St Giles."

"I have been sent to Rosemary Street. It must be here somewhere."

"I suggest you go and look for it then if you're so sure. Now, stop bothering me and be off with you!"

He swiped his arm to bat her away like she was a pesky fly. Two streets later, she saw a policeman and asked for his assistance.

"No Rosemary Street here, miss."

"Are you sure?"

"Absolutely. I've walked this beat for years."

"I was given this address, though."

"Well, someone has sent you on a fool's errand, lass. Look around you. Do you think anything as cheerful as rosemary could be found in this warren of streets? Not even on a signpost, lass, not even on a signpost," he sighed.

Poppy was tired, and her back ached. She sank into a dark doorway. She realised that Mrs Tremarie had tricked her, but there was nothing she could do about it. She was on the street. Thankfully, she had a tiny amount of money. The only place in the city that was familiar to her was Jesse's inn. She would find her way there at sunrise. He might give her a room at a fair price, considering who she was.

*

Jesse knew what had happened the instant he laid eyes on Poppy.

"He dumped you, didn't he?" Jesse taunted, delighted that his prophecy had been fulfilled.

Poppy tried to retain her dignity. It was becoming increasingly difficult to blindly trust that Anthony Gresham would do the right thing by her.

"Not at all."

"Come now, lass, we all know the truth. Get off your high horse and admit it."

"I need a room. I have money."

"How much?"

"Enough for a while. It's none of your business."

"You have a little gold mine in your belly, lass, and you don't even realise it."

Poppy frowned.

"You told me that he was Lord Gresham, so you did. Now, no denying it. If you leave it all to me, we will make a pretty penny out of the swine."

"You can't do that," cried Poppy, "the country depends upon him to stop a war."

"Pah! You silly girl. He has really spun you a yarn, hasn't he. You're more stupid than I thought. His lordship is trying to keep your mouth shut."

"He would never do that. He loves me."

Poppy didn't want to show Jesse the letter yet. The man burst into deep, roaring, rich gales of laughter.

"Can you clean?" he asked when the laughter subsided.

"Of course."

"You stay in the room on the top floor if you are prepared to work for me."

Poppy was overwhelmed by Jesse's kindness, deciding he was not such a bad sort after all.

But Jesse didn't have a kind bone in his body. He was hatching a diabolical plan, and Lord Gresham's loss would be his gain.

16

THE HEIRS

Lady Maria Holshausen Gresham took no pleasure in announcing that she was going to produce an heir. Her husband's repeated violations had crushed her spirit. She begrudged that her child had been conceived so unlovingly. To spite him, she had already made up her mind that the child would be raised a Catholic. It would be a huge thorn in her husband's newly found political side, Westminster being such an advocate for the Church of England. Her denominational decision was bound to raise eyebrows in the establishment.

Maria broke the news to him at the dinner table.

"I will give birth to an infant in the spring," she told him coldly.

"Jolly, well done. At last," he replied sarcastically.

Maria's pregnancy was bittersweet for Anthony. He was happy to have sired a legitimate heir, praying it was a son, but he wished he could rid himself of miserable Maria. Living separate lives wasn't enough distance between them. She openly despised him, and any possibility of a truce had been ruined by his recently beastly behaviour toward her. That said, his approach had been successful, and she had finally begun to fulfil her motherly duty. He wondered if he should have been more assertive to begin with. Chapels and priests and her endless list of religious demands she had made of him were going to be in the past. He would manage his marriage on his terms from this point forward.

As much as Maria hated her husband, she was delighted to be pregnant. The last time she felt love for somebody else was when her grandmother was alive. She knew this child would fill a void in her dull, lonely life.

She was fascinated by the changes in her body and had read all the books she could find on pregnancy and childcare. Things were progressing well. Her Harley Street doctor told her that she was fit, well and strong enough to give birth to a healthy child. Maria was determined that she wouldn't have the servants or a nanny raise her child, but she would do it herself. She didn't want to miss one moment of the joy that the baby would give her. It would be the greatest compensation for putting up with her loveless marriage.

She had noticed that Anthony Gresham had become more aggressive toward her since the night he had first violated her. He had begun making demands upon her from the moment he had been appointed to his more senior political role. She wondered if the stress of the job itself or the need to pretend his life was perfect triggered his black moods.

As expected, Maria was the perfect hostess. He could never find fault with her ability to charm his colleagues and gain the admiration of politicians, both national and international. Moreover, he realised he was married to this beautiful, intelligent woman and would never hold half as much sway if it were not for her diplomacy.

What was unfortunate was that Maria's pregnancy constantly reminded him of Poppy. He didn't feel guilt for the problems he had caused the girl, but he did have reason to feel vulnerable, and Anthony Gresham didn't enjoy being vulnerable.

One afternoon after a particularly harrowing session in Westminster, Lord Anthony's valet knocked on his study door and announced that a man by the name of Mr Patrick Gallagher was there to see him.

Anthony felt a knot developing in the pit of his stomach. He knew full well what the visit would be about, and he wasn't looking forward to it.

Mr Harris, the valet, showed Patrick into the study. As always, he was smart and well-groomed. Moreover, he was becoming more good-looking as he became older. This irked Anthony who had suddenly started looking florid and wrinkled from the copious amounts of alcohol he was consuming to compensate for his unhappiness and growing sense of unease. He was going to be a round, paunchy man sooner rather than later.

"Good afternoon! This is a nice surprise," Lord Gresham greeted cordially, keen to keep up appearances in front of his staff.

"No, it's not," Patrick snapped. "After what you've done to me, you should be surprised to see me at all."

"That will be all, Harris."

The two men awaited his departure before continuing their argument.

"I have ensured that your job at the club is guaranteed, Patrick. What's the big problem?"

"Do you think I want to be associated with a lot of back-slapping old men who are congratulating me on getting a maid pregnant? You have lost your mind."

"Now, now, it's not all that bad. Keep your voice down, please."

"I have resigned from my position. I have no inclination to work for you or your sort."

"Quieten down. My wife is pregnant. I don't want to upset her."

"What about Poppy Patterson? You don't mind upsetting her. But, of course, she is poor. She has no value in your world."

> "Listen to me, Irishman. First, you must accept that the elite doesn't see the world as you do."

Patrick Gallagher reached over the table and grabbed Anthony Gresham by his collar. There was a ripping sound as the shirt tore.

> "There is nothing elite about you. You're a disgrace. I am not your pawn. You play with people's lives as though you are a god. You're not playing with my life. I won't allow it."

Patrick pushed the man back. Anthony rocked on his heels, lost his balance, and crashed into the chair behind him. His eyes flashed as angrily as a barking German shepherd.

> "And another thing—you will address me as Mr Gallagher. I am no longer your friend. If I find you are trying to besmirch my good name again, I will get my lawyers onto you."

Anthony Gresham was humiliated but dared not say a word for fear that he would get punched again. A black eye would mean more scandal. He sat sulking.

Patrick left the study satisfied that he had clarified his intentions. If Lord Gresham involved or implicated him in any more nefarious activity, there would be hell to pay.

Mr Harris escorted Patrick to the entrance hall. The Irishman was surprised to see the lady of the house arranging an urn of flowers.

"Ah, good afternoon," she greeted politely. "If I remember correctly, you are Mr Gallagher from the club?"

"Yes, I am,"

Maria studied him. He was a good-looking man, and from the lilt in his voice he was southern Irish and probably a Catholic. He automatically rose in her estimation.

"I heard quite a commotion coming from the study," she pried.

"Indeed, there was a commotion."

"It must have been grave to warrant so much discord."

Patrick was not a politician, and he got to the point quickly.

"Lady Gresham, all you need to know is that your husband is lucky I didn't biff him on the nose."

Lady Gresham smiled broadly.

"Believe me, Mr Gallagher, it would have given me great pleasure if you had."

The comment caught Patrick off guard, and he began to laugh.

"Good day, Mr Gallagher," she trilled, her eyes radiating sincerity. "It has been a pleasure to see you again."

Patrick Gallagher chose to walk back to the St Regis Club. He needed fresh air and time to mull over the grave situation that he had found himself in. He refused to work in a position where he was being both protected and persecuted by Lord Gresham. It was an insult for him to be retained on the man's terms. He was glad he had taken a stand before the committee to tender his resignation. Everything in the world of the powerful patrons of the St Regis club was a sham. Many an old man had given him a good pat on the back and a wink for impregnating a maid, yet Patrick found the suggestion repugnant.

In the world of the wealthy, the truth didn't matter. No matter how many times you swore your innocence, it would be disbelieved. There was a web of hypocrisy and deceit that permeated the annals of the club. It was so deeply embedded in the institution's culture that any form of morality was a foreign substance.

*

After his resignation, Patrick wrote a letter to Sophie explaining that he had had no relationship with Poppy Patterson. He denied participating in any of the sordid events he had been accused of by the cruel-tongued gossips. He trusted nobody to deliver such an important letter, and asked Mr Aldridge to hand it to her when he paid Sophie her wages on Saturday evening.

Sophie was not surprised to receive it. She anticipated what it would read even before she opened it. Lies.

Although she was sad and disappointed to be handed the note, she was still anxious to see what it said.

She thanked Mr Aldridge and then casually meandered to her room, the envelope shoved deeply into her skirt pocket. She didn't want anybody to realise that she had received correspondence. They would all guess it was from Patrick, and the speculation of what it might say would add to her burden.

She sat on her bed and opened the letter. It was short and concise. Her premonition about its contents was correct.

Dearest Sophie,

I can't begin to imagine how tough life must be for you at the moment. I hope this letter gives you some comfort at such a difficult time.

Please believe me when I say there is a conspiracy led by the real father to discredit me. I have never been in a relationship with Poppy, and I say emphatically that the child is not mine.

There is pressure for me to 'make an honest woman of her' when neither she, nor the bairn, is my responsibility.

As you know, I am aware of how hard it is to be a lone parent after my poor mother's experience. I trust you know I am a good enough fellow to never leave my flesh and blood to the mercy of the parish, were it really the case.

I promise I didn't lie. I told you I am falling in love with you.

Sophie was desperate to believe what she was reading. At the same time, she wouldn't be made a fool of. She remembered how Poppy had alluded to her carnal knowledge of Patrick, and she had no reason to lie if they had feelings for each other. Why would Poppy want Patrick to run off with her? It was better to speak up and keep him for herself?

Sophie knew she would be a fool to believe what Patrick Gallagher had written in the letter. Actions spoke louder than words, and she'd known Poppy for far longer. The silly girl might have been a bit wayward and a dreamer, but she was never a poisonous liar. Anyone could claim to be innocent, but he would never be able to prove it. Not now. The gossip told her there was too much smoke for there not to be a fire. She couldn't commit to a relationship with a man where the question of his loyalty would haunt her.

Sophie was taken aback when she read the last few paragraphs.

To put clear water between me and this sorry business, I have resigned from The St Regis Club. I want no further dealings with a place that condones such awful manipulation and abuse of a female staff member.

All I can hope for is that you will give me the benefit of the doubt and trust me until I can to share the whole truth with you. I beg you to see me on your next day off to give me a chance to explain in person.

Yours forever,

Patrick.

After reading the letter, Sophie decided that he'd been sacked and this was an idiotic last-ditch attempt to fool her. Sophie took the note and shoved it through the fire grate. She watched it disintegrate. From that point forward, she would no longer think about Patrick Gallagher or a future with him. She was lowly laundry maid, she had no formal education, and she came from a lonely, impoverished part of England. He would soon tire of her once he had conquered her like he did Poppy. She had only a few days left to work at the club before leaving for Langford Manor. It would be a new beginning for her, and she would be able to revive her spirits in the joyful atmosphere of the happy Langford clan.

*

17

BLACKMAIL

Jesse knew the most direct way to lay hands on Anthony Gresham's immense wealth would be through Poppy. That was why he treated her with all the care in the world. Poppy was the goose who would lay the golden egg and would be treated as such until the moment it was laid.

One evening Poppy was feeling particularly bleak. Jesse invited her to his room with the sole objective of gaining her trust. He sat on a threadbare chair and went about the serious business of converting her into his disciple.

> "You've been the victim of frightful injustice, petal. I am fuming that Lord Gresham had been conniving and tricked you into his bed."

The more Jesse had her ear, the more Poppy was beginning to come round to his way of thinking. Everything that Jesse said was true.

Then he became deliberately provocative.

> "As the mother of his child, you deserve to be living far better than you are right now. He's got enough in his coffers to get you a nice little place

and some spending money. It's not cheap bringing up a child."

He left Poppy to ponder for a moment.

"Have you seen any talk of war in the newspapers?"

He spread out a carefully curated stack of them in front of her.

"None of these headlines scream impeding international doom to me? How about you?"

"No," Poppy replied meekly.

Spotting a slight crack in Poppy's devotion to her beau, Jesse spent a good few minutes labouring his point to shatter her dedication to him altogether.

"I reckon you should ask that Lord Greyson for a bit of money. Make things a bit easier for you?"

Poppy looked stunned.

"Don't worry. I'll help you," Jessie advised with a treacherous grin. "We'll keep it discreet. You're only asking for a bit to help with bed and board. It's not like blackmail, now is it?"

Poppy wasn't sure what blackmail was, so she hoped she picked the correct response and shook her head.

"Good girl. Now, I'll leave you to sleep on it. We can talk again in the morning. Let me help you upstairs. You look exhausted."

After another dismal night in the cold and damp Doggett Arms Inn, Poppy was keen to secure some creature comforts, now they seemed more within her grasp. Over breakfast, Jesse continued the manipulation of his prey.

"Of course, a rich man like Gresham might think he can ignore you. So, if you wanted a bit more money, you could threaten to tell his wife? Or a journalist? They're always open to publishing a saucy scandal. That would focus his mind while he drifts around that nice pad of his in Mayfair. Have you ever heard the phrase '*injured party?*'"

The more discomfort and loneliness Poppy felt, the more easily open she was to Jesse's suggestions. Once he had explained what an injured party she thought she definitely was one. Her appetite for recompense swelled as much as her belly.

Poor Poppy didn't understand what extortion was, nor blackmail. Before the morning was out, Jesse had led her into a far more dangerous situation than she was already in.

"Here you go."

He handed her some bread and cheese and a sugary hot mug of tea, and then he watched her eat for a while before making his final strike.

"Lass," Jesse crooned gently and with all the care in the world, "I will help you. You and the baby will always have a place here, and you will move to a better place as soon as you are on your feet. Why should he live in a mansion, and you live in this tatty old inn? This is no place to raise your child."

"He will be furious. His temper scares me."

"No need to be afraid, lass. He has more to lose than you do. Just do what I tell you and go about your business. You will be wealthy in no time at all. Best of all, my darlin', I will be here to protect you. You'll be fine."

"Thanks, Jesse. I'd be lost without you," Poppy said as she licked her finger to gather up the rest of the crumbs on her plate.

"You might want to see the society pages in London Gazette. It's a photo of Lord Gresham and his wife at a posh party at the palace."

Poppy looked at the lavish setting and the smiling couple with their arms linked at the elbow. The contrast between their life and hers at the Doggett Arms with Jesse was palpable. As her eyes skimmed the image, unconsciously, her jaw clenched ever tighter.

*

Lady Maria had two passions. The first was her newly conceived child, and the second the Catholic Church. When she was in London, she attended mass every morning at the same time. Her carriage would exit the courtyard of the Mayfair mansion promptly at nine o'clock every morning. She would go to church to say mass and then return at ten o'clock. Highly disciplined, she never broke her routine.

As her carriage turned from the lane behind her house into the street, she caught a quick glimpse of a woman standing across the road. The person wore an oversized coat. The coat was covered with a shawl, and a scarf covered her head. It was unusual to see somebody dressed in that manner in Mayfair. More remarkable was that the curious woman was staring at her house. If Maria had only seen her once, she would easily have forgotten the person, but she saw the woman standing in the same place earlier that week. Both mornings the person was in the same position watching the house, and Maria began to feel uncomfortable. Then, on the third morning, after church, Maria was escorting her husband to the Houses of Parliament. As they pulled out of the drive, the huddled figure stood there again. Maria pointed out the woman.

"It's odd. That woman has been standing in front of the house for some days. I feel like we are under surveillance."

"Perhaps I should send my valet to the police station and report her," Anthony said haughtily, not even bothering to look up from his papers.

"You can't report someone for standing on a public pavement," argued Maria.

"You forget who I am, Maria. I can do anything that I like. For example, I could lodge it as a security concern. That way, the woman will be chased away."

"There is that, of course, but perhaps she is looking for somebody. Perhaps one of her relatives works in our house?"

"Very well, Maria, I shall leave you to solve the problem. You're right. It is troublesome. Make sure the vermin are chased off the street."

Maria was a hard-hearted woman, but her bible told her to care for the poor. Her husband's arrogance was distasteful, but then again, she found everything about Anthony Gresham unpleasant these days. Earlier in their marriage, she had hoped they would take a liking to each other, but to no avail. Personally, he wasn't a devout Anglican and could have secretly changed religions. He wouldn't be the first prominent figure to do that. But he chose not to, just in case it was leaked and his precious political career was derailed. His selfishness saddened her greatly.

The following morning Lady Maria saw the woman again. This time she called for the coachman to stop. She opened the window of her cab and greeted the onlooker.

"Good morning, miss."

Closer up, she saw that the pretty young woman wasn't fat but pregnant. An expectant mother herself, Maria felt a connection with the woman and approached her with kindness, congratulating herself that her empathy with the deserving poor was one of her better traits.

"M'Lady," said Poppy with a curtsey.

"You have been standing opposite my home for quite some time. Are you looking for somebody?"

"Err, yes," replied a flustered Poppy, not expecting to speak to Anthony's wife.

"Who is it?"

Poppy was dumbstruck.

"Is it one of your relatives?"

The girl nodded.

"Well then, you can't stand on the pavement and hope they see you. Go to the courtyard and ask for our housekeeper, Miss Hopkins. She will help you."

Poppy put on a show of gratitude.

"Thank you! Thank you!"

"Very well, then. Good luck to you."

The coach rumbled off to church, and Poppy plucked up the courage to make her way to the back of the house as Lady Maria had instructed. The door was opened by a reserved but kind woman. Poppy mentally rehearsed her spiel one more time as Sally Hopkins appeared. The woman had bright pink cheeks and two plaits hanging out of her bonnet.

"Who do you want to see?" Sally asked warmly. "Have you come about the scullery maid job?"

"No. The master of the house. His wife said I must ask for him," Poppy lied.

"That's odd. Even Lady Maria has to make an appointment to see him."

"Oh," Poppy said disheartened. "She'll be quite angry if I don't pass on the message from the priest. I'm a cleaner at the church. He sent me just now."

The housekeeper felt sorry for her being sent out in such bitterly cold weather. It must be something urgent for the priest to send a female messenger.

"Oh, I see!" Sally declared. "I will try and call his valet. Perhaps he can help you."

Poppy was starting to enjoy the game. She had not deliberately stalked the house. She had just been too terrified to approach it. For once, Lady Luck had smiled up on her and made sure that Maria Gresham had noticed her and sent her to Sally Hopkins.

Merriweather was annoyed when the housekeeper interrupted his engrossing conversation with one of the footmen. Miss Hopkins was of the latest generation of bold and fearless women, and it was not unusual for

Sally to ignore protocol. Yet, as much as she drove him up the wall, he was also fond of the energetic young woman who moved like a whirlwind about the staid old house.

> "Mr Merriweather, sir, I have an urgent matter down in the courtyard."
>
> "What now, Miss Hopkins? How many times must I warn you not to interrupt me when I am busy?" he censured.

Sophie took him by the arm and steered him away from the footman.

> "There is a girl out the back who wishes to see the master. Lady Maria sent her to me, and now I have come to you so that you can—"
>
> "I understand. Take the girl discreetly to the coat room, and I will see her there. Do you know who she is?"
>
> "No, I didn't ask."

Merriweather rolled his eyes. It was so typical of Sally Hopkins to relay only half a story.

*

The valet reached the coat room and greeted Poppy. She was almost unrecognisable under all the winter garments. As well as looking familiar, she was looking a little heavy too. Shock and surprise made him terse.

"What are you doing here, Poppy?" He said, neither rude nor welcoming.

"I have come to see Lord Gresham."

Poppy was in the lion's den, but she was gaining confidence.

"We can't interrupt him. He has serious business. What's the matter? Is it something about the St Regis?"

"Well, I may as well show you. Everyone will find out soon enough."

Poppy pushed her shawl aside and unbuttoned her coat. Merriweather spotted the significant bulge of her stomach.

"Oh dear, so the gossip was all true," Merriweather said. "I had a feeling this wouldn't be Gallagher's handiwork. Far too principled—."

He stopped short of adding, *'unlike my master.'*

"Yes. And I want to see the master, or I will go to the newspaper."

Merriweather was a mature man who knew his gift of performing miracles was limited. This was one problem he wouldn't be able to solve for his master.

*

Merriweather took Poppy Patterson out into the courtyard and escorted her to the stables. The stable manager had a desk in a small office, but the man was out for the day. Merriweather believed it would be the ideal place to leave Poppy while informing Lord Gresham of the impending catastrophe.

Poppy was surprised that it had been so easy to get into the very space where her lover and father of her child resided. She also realised that Lady Maria was a reasonable woman who had shown her kindness instead of chasing her away like a dog. The pang of guilt was somewhat difficult to ignore.

Poppy and Jesse had worked out the plan to perfection. Lord Gresham would pay her weekly, and she and Jesse would share the spoils. Jesse had agreed that she could keep the child on his premises, and they would stick to the public story that the father was a sailor. Jesse was to clean up and modernise the room she lived in, and as long as she brought in a steady income, she would be welcome. The innkeeper was no better than a pimp.

*

Anthony Gresham was annoyed when Merriweather told him that there was someone to see him in the stables.

"By Jove, Merriweather, why do I employ a stableman?"

"It is not about the horses, sir."

"Well, what then?"

"I hate to say it, sir, but young Poppy Patterson from the club is in the manager's office and she's threatening to cause mayhem if you don't speak to her."

Anthony Gresham's thoughts began to run amok. The idea that Poppy was in such close proximity to his wife was a disaster. Then he remembered Maria mentioning a woman who stood watching the house for several days. *'That was her! Plucking up the courage to knock. The conniving shrew!'*

"Get her off my property, Merriweather," Anthony seethed.

"I don't think that's for the best, sir. She is threatening to go to the newspapers if you don't see her forthwith."

Anthony knew he had no choice but to face his former lover, and the less of a show he made, the better. It was sufficient an embarrassment that Merriweather was involved. It didn't have to be the kitchen and the stables as well. The sooner he saw her, the sooner she would be gone—hopefully for good, if he was sufficiently menacing.

*

The instant Anthony Gresham saw Poppy's face, he began to perspire. He tried to remain composed.

"How did you get in here?"

"Your missus told me to waltz right in," Poppy said cheekily.

"How much do you want?"

"Aren't you going to ask about your child?"

"It's not mine."

"Then why are you offering me money to go away?"

"You know I love you, Poppy," he began with the same old flannel.

"Oh, shut your trap, you snake!"

"Calm down."

Anthony closed the office door hoping nobody would hear Poppy's raised voice. It was going to be quite a task to get her to calm down. He gave listening to her a go.

"I want money from you every week," Poppy demanded. "I want you to look after me for the rest of my life."

Anthony wiped the sweat off his forehead.

"Of course, I was going to suggest that."

"I want the child to live in a nice house and attend a good school."

Poppy was playing one good hand that fate had dealt her, one powerful card at a time.

"You what?"

"I want you to buy me a house and have servants just like yours."

"Yes, yes, anything you want. Where can I find you?"

"The Doggett Arms Inn."

Anthony Gresham's heart skipped a beat. Poppy could never have thought up this idea by herself. He felt lighter. His problem was not going to be as big as he imagined. Now that he knew who was behind the scheme to blackmail him, it would be much easier to snuff the threat out.

"Yes, of course. You will have everything my wife has. I have always planned to look out for you. But you must leave as quickly as you can. If my wife finds out about this, she will ensure you receive nothing."

Poppy was not about to take the risk of getting nothing, and she chose to comply. She had a brief moment of weakness before she left.

"I love you, Anthony. I love you so much," she whelped as tears ran down her face.

"Be strong, my dearest, darling Poppy. I wish things could be different. Be patient. One day we will be together. It's kismet. I just know it. In the meantime, I will help from afar, my love."

He looked into her eyes, wiped away her tears, and then gave her a gentle shove out the door.

"Be quick now. Maria will be home any moment."

*

Merriweather discreetly escorted Poppy off the property, his head spinning like a barn owl, looking out for anyone spying on them. He felt reasonably confident that nobody had seen the expectant girl.

Anthony Gresham's thoughts turned to Jesse. The knowledge of the puppet master's identity was precious to him. He had already formulated a plan on how he would nip this little problem in the bud. It was simple, Jesse was greedy, and Anthony would exploit it.

18

THE DOGGETT ARMS

Later that evening, Lord Gresham donned simple clothes and chose to take a casual drive to a more colourful part of London. He had been there before and jostled through the masses on the wharf as if he belonged. He made his way until he found the narrow alley which led to the Doggett Arms. He rued the day he had brought Poppy to the filthy little ruin. He had never counted on either the likes of someone like Jesse to recognise him, or that Poppy would tell Jesse everything. He would have to be cunning if he wanted to rid himself of them.

When Jesse lifted his head and saw Lord Anthony Gresham standing before him, he showed no fear. If Anthony could have read his mind, he would have known that the man was terrified. Of all the people in the world, he didn't expect to see to see the lord standing before him.

All credit to Jesse, he put on a great show of bravery by acting blasé and brash.

"Your lordship," he guffawed. "What an honour to have you in my humble establishment."

"Let's get to brass tacks, Jesse. I am not here to be your friend or patronise your business."

"Of course, sir. You are far too good for the likes of this humble tavern."

"Poppy Patterson told me she is staying here with you."

"Not with me, your lordship. She sleeps in the next-door room. I would never infringe on your property," Jesse teased. "Although, I don't see much of her. She's exhausted carrying your bairn."

Seeing the greedy innkeeper chuckling ratcheted up Anthony's viciousness another notch.

"If you want money from me, you had better be more discreet old chap," Anthony told him.

Jesse's ears pricked up when he heard the word money.

"Yes, guv, jokes aside now, I am not out to cause trouble, so I'm not. I don't know what's gotten into her, but she told me she was going to get money out of you. Thinks she has you over a barrel, so she does. I warned her, guv. I warned her that there would be trouble."

"Good for you, Jesse, I always took you to be a sensible fellow," Anthony noted with a smile.

"Thanks for that, guv," Jesse beamed.

"Now, let's have some pints, Jesse. I can't come here and not have a pint."

Jesse was in his element. He couldn't believe such an esteemed politician would drink in his pub. Anthony didn't feel that the situation was ideal. Jesse had a big mouth and would tell everyone that a member of the establishment would have had a pint with him. On the flip side of the coin, Jesse was known for being a bit of an idiot, often succumbing to exaggeration and ideas above his station, and nobody would believe him.

For every pint that Anthony drank, Jesse drank two. The grog kept coming until Jesse was pretty stewed and eating out of the palm of Anthony's hand.

"Have you ever thought of opening a little pub in a large bustling city in one of the colonies?" Anthony asked.

"Why, guv? Where would I get the money for that?"

"With my connections with the colonies, Jesse, you can go to Sydney, Jamaica, even Hong Kong if you choose to. You can make a mint overseas. I can sort out your passage and give you some money to get you settled in your new home. And you know how much ladies love a man with an exotic foreign accent."

"Really?"

"Really. Oh yes. I can make the whole thing easy for you. Sponsor you, let's say?"

"You would do that for me?"

"Of course, Jesse, we are friends, and you sell the best ale in London."

Anthony was enjoying his sycophantic toying with the man.

"Of course, I can only fund a place for one person. That leaves a little problem, or perhaps two, if you catch my drift?"

"Ah. Yes."

"Yes. That indeed."

Anthony put on a serious face.

"She's been a curse since I met her, Jesse. Couldn't wait to get out of her clothes and seduce me. Pulled me onto the rocks like a siren with her charms. Now look at her. She can ruin me. She came to threaten me this morning, can you believe it? I had to do everything in my power to keep Maria from finding out. And when she does—"

Gresham made a slitting gesture along the front of his neck.

"No more money for our little venture. She'll take me to the cleaners."

"Now, now, let's not talk like that. We—I—can take care of little details like that."

"Good. That wretched bairn is a problem. Especially when she's making out it's mine. I mean who else might she have seduced at the club. Plenty of men stay overnight. What's to say she's not blackmailing them too. It's a mess."

"It is."

"Since she persisted with it being mine, I told her to get rid of it, but she defied me. I wish she'd slipped over on the cobbles in my courtyard. That would have put an end to her demanding money with menaces. "

"Perhaps I can help you, guv. My sister has helped a few women with a similar problem. She knows a doctor who is a bit easy with his prescription pad, let's say."

"Really. I thought men like that were a myth. Seems some are a bit more relaxed with the Hippocratic oath, after all, Jesse. Well, I never!"

Lord Anthony Gresham was playing Jesse like a fiddle.

"Let me have a word with my sister. I'll be in touch as soon as I know. All hush, hush. You know me. Since I prepare Poppy's food, it should be easy to slip her something from the doc."

"Well, I'm glad that's settled, Jesse. I shall sleep more easily tonight, my brother."

Gresham clapped hands on Jesse's shoulders and squeezed them with feigned gratitude.

"I think I'll have another pint, then be on my way."

Anthony Gresham left the inn in the early morning hours with Jesse, reassuring him yet again that he could rid Poppy of the child without her knowing.

"So, where will you be heading off to then? Decided yet?"

"Jamaica sounds like an excellent place to live. The sailors down the docks say it's hot there, and beer and rum flow like water."

"An excellent choice. I shall make some enquiries tomorrow to get things moving. Here's five pounds for your troubles. And your discretion, Jesse."

Anthony Gresham was delighted. What a relief it would be for Jesse would be wealthy and very far away. *'With any luck, the man will drink himself to death with all that rum'.*

Jesse couldn't get to sleep after Lord Gresham left. His mind was conjuring up images of his new life. All he had to do was make good on his promise to rid Poppy of the child in her belly.

*

In the morning, still a bit tipsy from the night before, he grabbed his coat and hat off the peg and shouted out a cheerful goodbye to Poppy, still jolly in the face of the heinous crime he would soon commit.

Jesse walked to the Seven Dials area. He arrived well before sunrise and waited until he saw the first fires in the gipsy camp. Then, he crossed into the square and approached a man who was boiling water in a cast iron pot on the open fire. The man was a tinker. Jesse put on his best smile.

"Morning, fella."

"What do you want?"

The tinker was brash. Jesse didn't know what else to ask for.

"Medicine," he blurted out.

"We can't help with that," the tinker joked, pointing toward Jesse's groin.

"God bless us," said Jesse. "No, my chap is just fine. It's a woman's ailment."

"Ah," said the tinker, "I think I know which ailment you mean."

"Well? Can you help? Or not. I've got cash on the hip here, sonny."

"You all come here for medicine. We are good for Roma medicine when you need it," the tinker said wryly. "Then you go back to hating us."

"Yeah, mate. Whatever you say. Will you get on with it now?"

The tinker glared at him.

"Go and see Ethel. Caravan with the green door."

He nodded towards it.

Jesse sensed rather than knew that the gipsy would kindly slit his throat from ear to ear if he crossed him, and he was glad to be walking away.

The innkeeper could smell the herbs before he reached the door. He could imagine the woman cooking up a bat, a frog and a few red toadstools.

He knocked gently on the door feeling a sense of trepidation. The door opened fast and banged against the caravan with an earth-shattering crash. Jesse got such a fright he jumped.

"Ethel?"

The woman looked down at him. Her wild grey hair was matted and stood about her head like a bush. Her face was almost yellow and lined with deep horizontal furrows. It was her eyes that were terrifying. They were small and yellow like those of an eagle, piercing and predatory.

"What?"

Jesse took off his cap and managed to look humble.

"I need medicine," he stammered.

Ethel looked at his crotch. Jesse shook his head. The woman beckoned to him to come in. A pungent smell permeated the caravan, a mixture of eye-watering ammonia and a sweet herb. It was revolting.

"What for?" Ethel demanded.

"My wife."

Ethel tilted her head to one side, a question in her amber eyes.

"She is with child," whispered Jesse. "We can't afford to keep it. And she nearly died giving birth to the last one too. Petrified she is. I only want to help her."

Although he was managing to wing it, his typical bluster was dissipating fast, and soon he only felt fear. His tongue stuck to the roof of his mouth.

Ethel pointed to her stomach and moved her arms wider and wider.

Jesse interpreted that she wanted to know how far pregnant Poppy was, and he demonstrated with his hands as well. Ethel didn't hide her disgust, her tiny yellow eyes blinking and staring him down. Jesse could imagine her ripping out his throat with her teeth.

Ethel scratched in a cluttered cupboard and pulled out an old, rusted tea tin. She put two teaspoons of grey-green powder into a small bottle and mixed it with the boiling pungent liquid on the stove. Ethel had spent many patient hours grinding down mouldy rye and was glad to be finally profiting from her endeavours. The desperate ones always had deeper pockets.

Ethel held up her hand, fingers wide to show five.

"Shillings?" asked Jesse.

Ethel kept her hand aloft.

"Quid?"

Ethel just stared.

Jesse reached into his pocket for all the money that Lord Anthony Gresham had given him. It just covered the expense.

"Must I give it all to you?"

Ethel nodded.

"Can I put it into her food?"

Ethel shook her head, and her wild hair followed.

"Tea?"

Ethel frowned.

"Thing is, she doesn't know."

Ethel's nostrils flared, and she looked vicious. She reached out with thin knobbly fingers and tried to take the bottle back, but Jesse clutched it to his chest.

Terrified, Jesse bolted from the caravan, fell down the three wooden steps, righted himself and ran. He finally stopped running when he was three streets away from Seven Dials.

He calmed down and remembered why he was doing it. Suddenly Jesse was full of his bluster and bravado again, and he began to whistle as he walked back to the inn. He decided to put some in Poppy's food and her drink. *'That should do the trick.'*

*

Lady Maria was loathed to miss mass that morning. For the life of her, she couldn't understand why she felt so ill. She had been suffering with nausea in the mornings since she found out she was with child. All the books she had read said this was a normal symptom.

She had eaten nothing strange the night before, which was confounding. Clutching her aching stomach, she was becoming increasingly concerned that she could be suffering from typhoid.

She sent a message to her driver telling him to take the remainder of the day off because she was ill. That day, her afternoon confessional was out of the question.

Her servants conjured up an array of different home remedies and promised her recovery, but her condition didn't improve. Out of desperation, they fed her rosemary and ginger-infused gin. The cook swore that if it didn't relieve the pain, nothing would.

After suffering throughout the day, Maria sent for her doctor.

The thin, bespectacled Dr Godwin was revered as the best physician in London. Maria wouldn't have settled for anything less.

"This is your first child, Maria, which means, unfortunately, you have no experience. You will need to be more robust in this situation. Do not be oversensitive to every ache and pain."

Maria glared at him.

"I have been suffering pain all day. This is not normal. I can assure you I can tell the difference between a twinge and a serious issue."

"Now, now, my dear, don't upset yourself."

Dr Godwin removed a small bottle from his bag and put it on the bedside table.

"Where is Lord Gresham at this time?" asked Dr Godwin.

"He has important business at the St Regis Club,"

"Best we don't disturb him. I am sure this tincture will do the trick."

Dr Godwin called Maria's maid to his side.

"You're to administer the drops to her every two hours. It will help her with the cramps."

The maid agreed. He leaned his head to the side and whispered his diagnosis.

"This could be a mild case of indigestion."

Maria twisted in agony as the man spoke.

"Is the baby well?" she asked.

"Of course, it is. Have you been riding lately?"

"No."

"Well then, my dear, there is nothing to worry about."

Dr Godwin felt annoyed. The aristocratic types were always overly sensitive and wanted constant attention. Hypochondriacs, the lot of them. He snapped his doctor's bag closed and made for his carriage in the courtyard. He desperately needed an ale after his trying time with Lady Maria.

19

GIVE ME THE BAG

The gate slammed behind her when Sophie Bryant exited the courtyard of the St Regis Club for the last time. On this happier occasion, she felt as if she had been liberated from a terrible prison not admitted to one, and a burden had been lifted from her shoulders. She carried the same battered suitcase that she had arrived with. She had gained nothing throughout her stay except what was left of her monthly wages after all the stoppages. There was just enough for the journey to the manor.

Sophie walked down the alley, and as she reached the street, she heard a man calling her.

"Miss Bryant," said the familiar lilting Irish voice.

Patrick Gallagher stepped out of the gloom, knowing this was his only opportunity to speak to her. He had felt like a spy as he stood in the shadows waiting for her to appear from behind the heavy iron gates, still with the ominous skull and crossbones etched on the sign above them.

"Whatever are you doing hiding in the dark?" she asked.

She witnessed embarrassment on his face.

"I have never done this before, and I'm not very good at it."

She wanted to laugh but didn't. Sophie kept quiet. She felt satisfaction at his discomfort.

"Where are you going?" Patrick asked, concerned, "Do you have a place to go to?"

"I am taking the late train from Kings Cross."

"Are you going home?"

"I don't think it's any concern of yours," answered Sophie.

"Fair enough."

He decided agreeing with everything she said was the best way to avoid angering her and making her run off.

"I have a cab waiting in St James Square. I will take you to Kings Cross."

"I would prefer to walk."

"Then I shall escort you."

Patrick and Sophie walked through St James Square.

"Please, give me the case,"

"I can carry my own case," Sophie said stubbornly.

"I know you can, but I don't want you to."

He gently prised the suitcase out of her hand. As his skin brushed against hers, he ensured it didn't again.

It was cold, and their breath formed two white clouds. The street lamps had yellow halos around them, and they could see the minuscule particles of mist floating in from the Thames in the air. Many of the side streets were almost empty because of the savagely low temperatures, save for a few optimistic beggars here and there.

As they left the more affluent area, the roads became busier and warm yellow light from pubs, coffee shops, and tobacco shops spilled onto the pavements.

"May I buy you something warm to drink?"

"No, thank you, Mr Gallagher."

Sophie was adamant that she wouldn't entertain any kind gestures from him. At the first coffee shop Patrick saw, he stopped and opened the door. He stepped inside and held the door open for her.

"I said no."

"I have your case," countered Patrick. "Where I go, it goes."

Sophie was furious with herself for handing him the case, yet at the same time, she wanted to be with him.

They sat down at a small table in the corner. Patrick ordered two coffees. They waited in silence until the waiter finally served it.

Patrick finally spoke, a deep desperation entering his voice.

"Sophie, I care for you very much and want you to be in my life."

Sophie was tired and disappointed. Everything was going wrong. She didn't want to go. She didn't want to stay. She did want to cry, though.

"I know that we have spent very little time together. But I still know you fill me with great joy. I know that I can make you happy too."

Sophie spoke for the first time.

"You're a lying silver-tongued snake," she accused him venomously. "Haven't you forgotten about Poppy?"

"I am not giving you a choice, Sophie Bryant. You will spend the rest of your life with me."

"And I will be haunted by Poppy and your love child."

"Stop this madness," he said, his voice holding authority.

Sophie stared down at the table.

"Do you think I would be here if that child belonged to me? After everything I told you about my mother's struggles? No child of mine would miss out on my love and protection—however it came into this world—I can assure you."

"I don't know how to take you."

"Look, Lord Gresham is responsible for spawning that child. He wanted to pay me to marry Sophie to take the heat off him. I said no. That's why I resigned. I didn't want to have anything more to do with him. That despicable offer finally killed our long friendship."

Sophie searched his face. His jaw was set defiantly, and he didn't take his eyes off her. She was almost convinced, but she wanted to hear the story from Poppy before she committed herself to Patrick. She hoped Poppy would do the right thing and come clean about who the father was, once and for all.

"I want to speak to Poppy."

"But I don't know where she is?"

"Someone must know?"

With reluctance, Patrick knew he would need to find Poppy to convince Sophie he was innocent.

"Alright, I will find her," said Patrick, "but you must promise me that you will stay in London until this mess is cleared up."

"My train leaves tonight," said Sophie.

"I will put you into a decent hotel and find Poppy. If you still want to leave after you have heard the truth will buy you another ticket. I will never keep you against your will. All I ask for is the benefit of the doubt for a day or two. Please?"

Sophie had enough faith in him to believe his plan was sincere. Deep in her soul, she knew she could trust Patrick Gallagher once they were free of the clutches of the St Regis club and its staff and clientele.

"Where will you begin searching?" asked Sophie.

"The St Regis."

*

Patrick ensured that Sophie was settled in a comfortable hotel on the better side of the city. By now, it was almost midnight, but he was determined to find Gresham. On a cold night like that one, cabs were few and far between, and he resigned himself to walking to the St Regis. At least it gave him time to think.

Patrick reached the club and climbed the steps toward the giant wooden doors that separated high society from their common compatriots. He banged the huge door knocker a few times to wake up the concierge, who was probably dozing on the job at that late hour. Within seconds the stately door was opened by a yawning concierge. The concierge was too tired to ask Patrick any questions. Besides, he was very fond of the young Irishman.

> "Evening, Mr Gallagher. Normally, I'd let you straight in, but since you don't work here anymore—"
>
> "Quite. Good to see you as diligent as ever, Mr Mitchell. Would you happen to know if my friend Lord Gresham is in residence? He should be."
>
> "Yes, sir. Been here for the whole week, I think."
>
> "Is he in his regular room?"
>
> "Yes, sir. I will get a post boy to push a note under his door."
>
> "No need. He's expecting me. Just double checking and all that."

Before Mr Mitchell could object any further, Patrick breezed past him, headed toward the staircase, and began climbing. The concierge was an older man who did not desire to chase Patrick up three flights of stairs with his arthritis. He found the cold winter weather was terrible for it.

Patrick reached the fourth floor. He turned into the vast corridor. When he reached Gresham's door, he banged loudly. He thought the noise would wake everybody on the floor, but the Irishman didn't care.

There was no reply.

Patrick banged again so hard the door rattled on its hinges. This time a few doors along the passage opened, and a few old men grumbled about the noise.

Eventually, Patrick gave the door a good hard kick, and it swung open. Everyone in the club knew something unusual was afoot. Those men still inside their rooms pressed their ears against their doors, desperate to find out more. They looked more like gossipy washerwomen than prominent members of society.

Patrick barged into the room. Anthony Gresham was standing, gripping a sheet against him to cover his loins. The rest of the sheet was draped over a startled, naked young woman, her black hair tousled.

Patrick ignored the girl and took long, determined strides toward Anthony. The young girl didn't understand what was happening and clutched more of the bedclothes around her.

Patrick grabbed Anthony by the throat and squeezed.

"Poppy Patterson, where is she, Gresham?"

Lord Gresham balled his fist and swung a punch at Patrick's head. It landed squarely on his assailant's temple, and the Irishman was dizzy for a moment. Through the haze, he launched himself at Gresham. The two of them went sprawling across the floor. Patrick landed on top of Gresham and sat on top of him. He swung at Gresham, happy to hit any part of the man that he could. Soon, Gresham's head began to spin, and he had no more passion for the fight.

There was a brief lull in the fighting while Patrick conducted his interrogation.

"Poppy Patterson, where is she?"

"Doggett's Arms, near Wapping."

Patrick got up off the floor. He straightened his clothes. Then he looked at the girl. She couldn't have been more than twenty years old.

"Get up and get dressed. Never see this man again. He will ruin you."

He didn't wait for a response from her. Patrick was sure that every member of the St Regis Club had their ears against their doors and had heard everything. By dusk, Lord Anthony Gresham would no longer be a high-ranking member of the British establishment.

*

Jesse had spent most of the day showing Poppy kindness and giving her a great deal of attention—unusually so. He had made her several cups of tea, and there was soup with her bread rather than cheese. She was touched when he told her that she could go to bed early because she looked exhausted.

Throughout the day, Jesse slowly administered Ethel's drops to Poppy without her knowledge. He was becoming impatient because nothing seemed to be happening, and Poppy was as right as rain. He doubled, then tripled the dose. Nothing.

Finally, at midnight he decided that the old gipsy woman had tricked him. He was silently fuming when he heard the creak of the rickety staircase.

Poppy was standing on the landing, sweaty, weak at the knees and clutching her nightgown at her sides.

"What's wrong, petal?"

"I think the baby's coming, Jesse!"

"It's much too early for that love. You've got another month to go, didn't we say? Go to bed and get some rest. You'll be right as rain in the morning."

"There is something wrong, Jesse. I know it."

"Would you like me to sit with you for a while? I can bring you a cuppa. Take your mind off it?"

"Thank you, Jesse. You're too kind."

"No trouble at all. You get yourself settled."

Poppy returned to bed, but her stomach was heavy, like she was carrying a dead weight.

20

CALL DR GOODWIN

Morning dawned clear and calm. There was no wind or cloud, and the black smoke that plagued London was miraculously gone. For most, this was a good omen for the day. The fresh, crisp air did nothing for Patrick Gallagher's mood. He was exhausted. At least at that hour, the cabs were back on the streets, and with a mile to go, he managed to wave one down. He gave the man directions to the hotel where he had left Sophie.

The hotel was small and clean. The copper was pristinely polished, and the small parlour and dining room were spotless. Patrick Gallagher asked the manager to tell Sophie that he was there.

Sophie had not slept a wink. Her mind had been too busy mulling over yesterday's events. She appeared in the lobby within minutes of Patrick calling for her.

"You look a sight for sore eyes," he said, smiling when he saw her tousled head.

"I couldn't sleep," she murmured.

Patrick thought about how beautiful she was so early in the morning.

"Have you found Poppy?"

"Yes and no. I have an address. I thought we should go together. If you'll agree, that is. It's the only way we can put your mind to rest. I just know it. One quick conversation, and we'll have this all straightened out."

Patrick paid the hotel manager. He picked up Sophie's battered suitcase. He was beginning to hate the horrid thing. He would buy her a new one, one that matched his.

"She is at an inn called the 'Doggett's Arms.'. It's off the wharf at Wapping."

"Is she well?" asked Sophie, concerned.

"I don't know, Sophie. Anthony Gresham neither knows nor cares."

*

Lady Maria had struggled through the night, but by sunrise, it was clear she was losing the cherished child she had waited so long to conceive.

Anthony arrived home just after dawn, looking as if he had slept in his clothes. He was aware of the commotion around his wife's bedroom but had not bothered to ask what was amiss.

He was home for approximately an hour when Merriweather told him the doctor had been called a second time for Maria.

"That woman is impossible. I dare say she will behave like a spoilt princess for the duration of this confinement."

"Do you wish to speak to her maid?" asked Merriweather.

"No, Merriweather. If it matters that much, you go see her. Come back with some decent information, if there is any, and not more *'women's issues'* tittle-tattle."

Merriweather was surprised by Lord Gresham's bad manners. They usually got on very well. Merriweather knew nothing was the same since Poppy had won the upper hand over Anthony Gresham in his own home.

The valet walked to the wing which housed Lady Maria's bedroom. As he reached the landing, he saw Dr Godwin enter Maria's room again.

"What is happening here?" Merriweather asked young Sally.

"I am not sure. We believe there may be something wrong with the child. It wasn't the lady imagining it. I think it's serious."

Merriweather was shocked.

"Are they both distressed or just the child? What does her maid say, Sally?"

"She says her ladyship is very tired and in great pain."

"When did this start, then?"

"All day yesterday and through the night."

"Did someone not think to call Lord Gresham from the club?"

"Yes, sir. We did, we sent a messenger, but he was told that his lordship was busy with important matters and not to be interrupted."

Merriweather was disgusted. He had a good idea of what his boss was so busy with he would not come home. Every time he had given Merriweather the night off, it usually meant that he didn't want his valet to know that he had another woman in his bed.

*

Jesse was used to Poppy being up at the crack of dawn. The sun was well up in the sky before Jesse decided to investigate his cash cow's condition.

"Poppy, lass? Where are you?" called Jesse in his kindest voice.

He opened the bedroom door and walked to the bed.

"Morning, lass, and how are you?"

"Not good, Jesse."

"Still under the weather, then?"

"Yes, me head hurts and me stomach aches," answered Poppy weakly. "Feels like I've been kicked by one of them footballers."

"Aww, lass. Let me call Mother Nel for you. She'll know what to do."

"Who's she?"

"Only the best self-appointed midwife to the area."

"Thank you, Jesse."

Jesse sent a messenger to call Mother Nel, then went off to make Poppy another cuppa. He poured the last few drops of Ethel's potion into it.

"She's on her way. I've made this to warm up your bones. It's chilly in here this morning."

Poppy looked at the ice that had formed on the inside and the outside of her pokey, single-glazed window. Then, Jesse held the cup while Poppy drank her tea.

"That's it, lovey. Drink it all down."

Jesse was smiling, not to reassure Poppy but because he knew it wouldn't be long before he was on a ship bound for the tropical paradise of Jamaica.

*

When Dr Godwin arrived at the bedside, Lady Maria was lying in a dark puddle of blood. She was as snow white as the sheets that covered her. Maria had developed cold chills, and she was severely weakened by the loss of blood. She had been bleeding since dawn, and it was obvious to all that she would lose the child. No medical training was needed.

Dr Godwin pulled back the bedclothes and stared at his patient. It was distasteful, but he would need to examine his patient properly.

"I need to have privacy," he told Miss Hopkins, the housekeeper.

"I am not leaving this room, doctor. You can carry me out if you must."

Dr Godwin lifted Maria's nightdress, and Miss Hopkins heard him gasp.

"What is it, doctor?"

"Call the chambermaid," he ordered. "She has lost the child. It will need to be disposed of."

Until that moment, Maria had not said a word. She was frail and struggled to sit up straight. She strained to pull her head down towards her chin and looked down at the sheet that she lay upon. Between her legs was a small, hard ball of fleshy tissue, the size of an egg, the poor child she had conceived with her husband.

Maria was too weak to shout, but Dr Godwin heard her clearly.

"My child will be buried, not tipped into a sewer. Get out now, or I will kill you when I am well."

Dr Godwin was about to say something, but Miss Hopkins cut him short.

"You heard her ladyship. Get out."

Maria felt as if her heart had been crushed in her chest. The maid sat beside her and stroked her employer's head. Sally Hopkins had the awful task of scooping up the foetus as her ladyship looked the other way.

"Ask Merriweather to fetch the priest, Sally. Father Luigi can conduct the service here, and then—"

Her rasping voice tailed off.

"Of course, ma'am."

The following day, Father Luigi promised to place the tiny human form next to Maria's grandmother in the family crypt and that the loving old woman would take care of the little one in the netherworld that awaits us all.

*

It was noon before Anthony Gresham bothered to see his wife. When he did, he was shocked at how his privileged life had disintegrated in a matter of hours. From the moment that Poppy appeared at the gate until now, nothing had gone smoothly.

Patrick Gallagher had found him in bed with a woman and then forced him to disclose where Poppy was. He had made promises and paid out money to Jesse to cover his track and deal with the loathsome child. And now, his wife Maria had miscarried his legitimate heir. That said, he couldn't understand why Maria was so bothered about it all. Granted, she felt ill, but the thing was hardly a person.

Something far more calamitous for him than losing his heir was that he knew his membership at the St Regis would be revoked. The scandal would be too much to recover from. No amount of money and manipulation would save him this time.

They didn't care whether his father was the founder or not. Anthony had disgraced himself. The St Regis would garner the reputation of a brothel, and that was unacceptable.

Anthony had no doubt that the Prime Minister would have stern words and dismiss him from the special committee. By midnight, the scandal would be in the newspaper. By noon, he would need to flee to the country to avoid the publicity. All this whirred around his head like a buzzard on the African plains.

*

Anthony pulled up a chair next to Maria's bed and sat down. As their eyes met, one lonely tear trickled down Maria's cheek.

"Dr Godwin says it's probably something you ate and will have no bearing on your reproductive capabilities in the future."

"Why are you here? You should be at the club or Westminster, where your heart truly belongs."

"I came home early to see you."

"But I didn't send for you?" Maria said softly.

"You did, my dear. You were in delirium."

"You're lying to me."

"Why would I lie?" he snapped.

"Because you always lie when it suits you. I have never trusted you, Anthony."

Lord Anthony Gresham was not in a position to control himself.

"If you had not been a cold, frigid woman, I wouldn't have spent all my time at the club. That's where the rot set in. Because of your beliefs. Now, I am not welcome anywhere."

"I was handed to you like a chattel. It was humiliating. I didn't love you, and neither did you me."

"Don't blame me for your father's actions."

"You could have said no. You didn't need to marry me. How could you expect me to behave like a loving wife under those conditions."

"And you wonder why I sneaked girls into the St Regis? Good grief. You're more stupid than I thought."

There was a long pause. Anthony realised he had said too much.

"Which girls? I want names."

"I can't remember them all, dear."

"Try."

There was a long silence. Maria's beleaguered brain shuffled through the pieces of the puzzle.

"That girl who came to visit. She was pregnant. Was she one of them?

"Yes. Poppy Patterson, I think?"

"What?"

"You don't need to be concerned about it. I have made plans to get rid of the child. There will be no embarrassment on that score. She won't speak out when she sees how difficult I can make life for her."

"How could you do that? Kill your own flesh and blood?"

"It matters not. It's probably dead already."

Anthony began to laugh darkly. At least one problem would be dealt with by the end of the day.

"And the girl, where is she now? What if she needs a doctor? Anthony! Answer me. You might be happy with this, but I am not! I won't have the death of three souls on my conscience. Tell the stables to get a coach ready for me."

"You're gravely ill. You can't travel. It will kill you."

"Then, I will crawl out of this room and tell Merriweather to do it myself."

Anthony Gresham watched his wife sit up slowly. She slowly slid her feet to the floor and held onto the bed for support. She shuffled to their bedroom door and opened it.

"Sally," she croaked.

The housekeeper came running to see what the matter was.

"What are you doing out of bed? You need to rest!"

"Tell the stables to get a coach ready, and then come and help me get dressed."

Maria went back into the room, pale and trembling. Her husband was sitting in a reverie, ignoring everything happening around him.

"Where is the girl now?" she asked.

Anthony seemed not to hear her.

"Where is Poppy Patterson?"

There was no response. Lady Maria Gresham looked as if she was on death's door, but as weak as she was, she was able to give her husband a good hard slap.

Battle-weary, Anthony Gresham had nothing left to lose. He told her the address.

Lady Maria was helped into the coach by her servants. Anthony, in his madness, got into the coach with her. Merriweather and Sally Hopkins climbed up next to the driver, pulling their winter coats up around their necks.

With a crack of the reins, their long trundle to Wapping began.

21

LOSS AND GAIN

Mother Nel gently wiped Poppy's face with a damp cloth.

"How is the child?" Jesse asked Mother Nel.

"The child is moving, and it's healthy," she announced before lowering her voice to a whisper. "As for Poppy, I fear she is close to death."

Jesse couldn't stand still and paced around in little circles. Something was desperately wrong. The mixture was not working as it should have. He had expected the child to come down, stone dead, hours ago. Instead, it was still strong, and the mother was the one in trouble. Lord Gresham would kill him if the plan went awry. Poppy's death was an unfortunate by-product of the deal that the two negotiators could tolerate, but the child's survival would be highly problematic to both of them.

*

Patrick and Sophie hurried down the wharf searching for 'The Doggett Arms.' It was slow going as the harbour was full of merchant ships abuzz with the activity of loading and unloading. Towards the more decrepit side of the wharf, an old sea dog they chatted to pointed to a dark narrow alley with the end of his pipe.

Sophie followed Patrick down the alley, and right at the end was a dirty little window and a door.

Patrick knocked at it loudly, and Jesse opened up with a grin. It had been a long time since the inn had seen wealthier patrons.

"Welcome to me, little lodge," he said, smiling at Patrick.

"Poppy Patterson, where is she?"

"What are you on about?"

"Cut the nonsense."

Patrick heard an agonised cry from one of the lodging rooms upstairs.

"It's her, I am sure it's her," cried Sophie. "Quickly!"

Patrick pushed a protesting Jesse out of the way and ran up the stairs with Sophie close on his heels. They crowded into the tiny room and saw Poppy limp and exhausted on the bed.

"Poppy!"

Sophie stood beside her friend and took her hand tenderly.

"Sophie, I knew you would come,"

Poppy smiled weakly, her eyes bleary and unfocused.

"I am sorry, Sophie. I am so sorry. I lied to you. I am so sorry."

Sophie felt her throat close up. Guilt, anger, and sadness welled up in her. Her eyes stung, and no words would come out when she opened her mouth.

"I deceived you. You need to know the truth."

Poppy was slipping in and out of consciousness. Jesse heard the clatter of more heels on the landing. He had never had so many people in the small inn at one time.

A beautiful ghostly woman was standing at the doorway, being assisted to walk by two servants. Behind was Anthony, uncharacteristically meek.

"Why are you here, and who are these people?" hissed Jesse, terrified of Anthony's retribution when he realised the wrong person could soon die.

"I am Lady Gresham," answered Maria.

Merriweather pushed Jesse aside.

"Have you no manners, man?"

"Why have you come here, Maria?" asked Patrick.

"My husband has plotted to kill the unborn child. I couldn't let that happen, but I fear I might be too late!"

Patrick caught Anthony's gaze and gave him a sinister look.

"Poppy is very weak," said Mother Nel, stating the obvious.

"Oh, how terrible," cried Maria, slumping down onto the bed with Sophie on the other side. "I must get this poor girl some help. Can't we get Doctor Godwin over? Get the driver to fetch him this instant."

She looked at the young woman and began to weep.

"I fear there is no time for that, ma'am," Sally whispered in her ear.

"If not for her, then the child? We must do something! I shall never, ever forgive you for this, Anthony!"

Poppy's unresponsive body was having severe contractions. Mother Nel elbowed her way in amongst the two women. She could tell Poppy lacked the strength and coordination to expel the infant herself. On what might have been the last contraction, Mother Nel pushed down on Poppy's stomach with so much force the contents of her womb started to spill out. She ripped back the covers preserving Poppy's dignity.

From where she was, Mother Nel could see the head of the child. She put her fingers around it as best she could and twisted a little, like a sommelier at the club would tease out a cork from a bottle of Bordeaux. A tiny wrinkled head appeared, and Mother Nel gently kneaded Poppy's stomach until the rest of the child slowly slithered out behind it.

Lord Anthony Gresham stood in the doorway watching the scene. His wife, whom he had always believed was as cold as steel, was sitting on the bed next to his dying lover, comforting and consoling her, showing her boundless compassion for others in need.

"I am so sorry that my husband has done this to you."

Maria stroked Poppy's forehead.

"Your baby is alive, and she is gorgeous."

Maria smiled gently.

"Do you want to see her?" the lady said, knowing there would be no response.

Maria took the child from the midwife and lay it on Poppy's bosom. It began to suckle.

"A girl," she whispered. "I will call her Poppy. After her mother."

Sophie watched from the side of the bed. It was the first time she saw Poppy at peace in many months.

Maria bent over and spoke into Poppy's ear. Nobody else could hear what she said.

"I will look after your little girl, Poppy. Don't you worry.."

Poppy's final breaths became more shallow until there were no more.

"The child is small but strong," said Mother Nel.

Sophie was filled with sorrow, and Patrick took her hand. The baby reminded her of little Ann, her tiny sibling who died next to Ada. Years of pain at the death of all those babies came crashing down upon Sophie, as did the demise of Poppy, always so bright and full of life, now limp and pale.

"What are you doing, Maria?" stammered Anthony Gresham, trying to grab the child.

Maria was weak but as defensive as a barking terrier standing its ground.

"I am leaving you, Anthony. I am leaving England. Baby Poppy and I are going to Austria, where we will live in peace."

"You can't leave me like this."

"Yes, I can. The law will take care of you, Anthony, and I will take care of the child.

"Mr Gallagher, make sure the innkeeper and my husband stay here. Mr Merriweather, ask the driver to take you to the police station."

*

When the dust had settled and Jesse Doggett and Lord Gresham were safely detained, Patrick Gallagher took Sophie by the hand and led her out onto the wharf. They began walking until they found a cab.

"Where to?" shouted the driver through the hatch.

Patrick squeezed Sophie's hand affectionately as he replied.

"To the Lyon's Tearooms Piccadilly, my good man. I think the lovely Miss Bryant here will find it the perfect place to consider a very important question."

Like The Runaway Laundress? Here are some more books in my 'Victorian runaways' series you'll love. Have you read them all?

- https://mybook.to/RunawayGirls

GET THREE FREE AND EXCLUSIVE EMMA HARDWICK BOOKS

These are all exclusive to my newsletter—you can't get them anywhere else. You can grab your free books on BookFunnel, by signing up here:

- https://rebrand.ly/eh-free

Hi! Emma here. For me, the most rewarding thing about writing books is building a relationship with my readers, and it's a true pleasure to share my experiences with you. From time to time, I write little newsletters with short snippets I discover as I research my Victorian historical romances, details that don't make it into my books. In addition, I also talk about how writing my next release is progressing, plus news about special reader offers and competitions.

And I'll include all these freebies if you join my newsletter:

- A copy of my introductory novella, The Pit Lad's Mother.
- A copy of my introductory short story, The Photographer's Girl.
- A free copy of my Victorian curiosities, a collection of newspaper snippets I have collated over the years that have inspired many of the scenes in my books.